One Lost Summer

Richard Godwin

Everything I knew ended then as she put the Dunhill to her lips. I can still see her slender fingers holding the cigarette just before the sniper blew away her hand. Her burning Diva Zippo fell to the ground. Then came the second shot, and I watched my reflection die in the fading light of her eyes. One lost summer that slow motion moment replayed itself forever in my mind. A key was turning in a lock. Over and over again.

NEW BEGINNINGS

1.

I remember.

I was sipping a highball, as I watched the removal men load the Pickfords lorry with the last of my boxes. The driver waved at me as I leaned against the doorway.

I raised my glass and watched them turn at the end of the road. I lingered on the threshold of my immaculate Richmond home. Then I passed along the empty corridors, and stood in the vacant rooms that held no memories.

I left my empty glass in the kitchen sink and removed my wallet from my pocket. I stared at the name on my credit card. Then I walked out into the burning street.

London was hitting the high 80's the day I moved, and that summer the temperature kept climbing. Pavements buckled, tarmac split. We were being given a glimpse through the cracks. I saw people break apart, tempers flare. It was like living beneath a magnifying glass. The city is never prepared for that kind of heat.

From what I recall, statistically, there were more assaults than previously recorded. But statistics do not concern me, nor do these incidental events. They were lost to me then. And while I may be interested in records, it is a different kind of memory I sought in those blazing months, when someone set a match to what I knew and who I was. I was left with only blindness and yearning.

I can't remember what I thought as I drove out of Richmond, away from the past. I stopped only once on the way to the new house, at a small pub where I drank a Glenfiddich. The men were getting out of the lorry as I pulled my Mercedes onto the neat gravel drive.

I'd arrived at my new life in Shepperton.

* * *

After they left I unpacked the box marked "Important Stuff". I removed my supply of whisky and wine, placing the 12 bottles of 1978 Montrachet in the Northland fridge. The house was perfect, from the quartz worktops, to the oak floors. It was all new, and some distant, suffocated part of my being began to breathe. I admired the suede wallpaper in the living room, looked out at the tree lined avenue, and passed through the French doors to the landscaped garden, and down the springy grass to the fountain at its end.

The water played out of Hermes' mouth like a liquid reel of film and the landscape turned to sepia for an instant when all the colour went out of the world. I turned away and went inside to inhale the odour of newness again. I was high on the tabula rasa feel.

As my wine chilled I scaled the stairs to the master bedroom. There was no history there. I entered the en suite bathroom, and found myself illuminated before the mirror, as the sensor lights came on.

I considered my even, expressionless face, the full head of silver streaked hair, and my watchful blue eyes hiding beneath the steel rimmed Gucci glasses that gave me a professorial air. I stood back and looked at my physique, slim, toned, for someone approaching fifty. I had the appearance of a man who played tennis. I wondered what green courts I passed my hours in, and with whom. I seemed an empty proposition, plundered and lost. And I thought about tomorrow, feeling the sweat crawl down my back like a hungry spider. I saw a shape move on the Villeroy and Boch tiles as I left my reflection there and found myself in the hallway. It seemed to lead nowhere and so I went downstairs, away from the shadow in the bathroom.

The agents had left a welcome basket in the kitchen, and a cheap bottle of champagne by some unknown estate in the fridge. I opened it, since the Montrachet was not yet chilled, and I thought how quickly the bubbles burst in the neck of the bottle and of the fragile nature of time. I tried to recall the feeling of hunger as I nibbled on a pear and some cheese, a basic cheddar from a supermarket, sweating in its plastic wrapper.

By now it was growing dark and the windows were full of the trees' shadows. They seemed unknowable, beyond my reach, and so I drew the curtains. A car was passing by with its windows down. I could hear the all too familiar, insistent opening notes of Fleetwood Mac's "The Chain". I blocked my ears as Stevie Nicks sang, "Damn your love, damn your ties".

I stood in the hollow room, my breathing laboured and exaggerated, as a nerve twitched in my right arm. Then I remembered what I'd packed in my case.

Nestled beneath my clothes was the 64 year old Macallan. I caressed the lost-wax casting and opened it, inhaling its violent oxygen.

2.

It was 90 degrees the next day. I showered and dressed, then left the house.

I was opening the door to my car when I heard my name called.

"Mr. Allen?"

I turned and froze.

She was standing on the edge of my drive in a floral print skirt and matching blouse, and she raised her sunglasses and looked at me with the purest translucent green eyes I'd ever seen. She seemed to have walked straight off a film set, and I looked around for the crew, seeing only the empty avenue.

"I believe you've just bought The Telescope," she said. "I'm your neighbour."

I walked over to her and extended a hand.

"I just got here last night, slept like a log, and still half asleep, forgive my slowness."

"Welcome to Broadlands Avenue. I thought I'd introduce myself, Mr. Allen, and ask your indulgence."

"Please, call me Rex."

She lowered her voice to almost a whisper.

"Rex, we're having a party tonight, it won't be noisy, but we don't want to disturb you. I'm sure you're busy unpacking, but I thought it would be a nice opportunity for you to meet the neighbours."

"What time?"

"Drinks around six?"

"Can I bring anything?"

"Just yourself."

She looked over my shoulder.

"It's a fantastic house, I've seen the work they did on it, although…"

"Something I don't know?"

"It's the only one round here with no swimming pool. I'd feel a bit cheated."

"I don't particularly like them."

"How odd."

"And the garden is fantastic."

"That's true."

"I wonder how it got its name."

"One of the previous owners was obsessed by astronomy, he had telescopes everywhere."

"That must have been a bit discomforting."

"Oh, I don't know, it depends if you've got something to hide. I like the SLK," she said, patting my Mercedes, "good body. See you about six then, and if you want to, bring your swimming trunks."

She was walking away when I said, "I didn't catch your name."

"How stupid of me, Evangeline. Evangeline Glass."

* * *

I did some grocery shopping, and spent the day unpacking boxes, stopping to eat a lunch of smoked salmon and to imbibe a bottle of the now chilled Montrachet. It was almost five when I stepped into the shower. I was careful not to rub my skin raw afterwards as I dried myself.

The house next door was secluded behind Beech hedges. I stood on the pavement and looked around. It was a long and silent avenue, punctuated only by the noise coming from the party. I heard female laughter as I rang the bell.

Evangeline answered the door and led me through to the kitchen. She was wearing a light blue sarong, wrapped tightly around her body.

"I brought you a couple of bottles," I said.

"Krug, how generous Rex. I think I'm going to like you."

She kissed me on the cheek and I watched her bend and place them in the fridge. I estimated she was in her early thirties, but her body was younger, full, and toned. I could smell melon rising from her tanned skin.

"Come and meet the neighbours," she said.

I put on my sunglasses and stepped outside into the glare.

By the pool a fat man in a beige jacket was talking loudly to a smaller guy in white shorts and a Miami shirt. Two women in bikinis were lying on loungers set against the back wall, while a swarthy man in a pair of faded jeans stood putting sausages on the barbecue with a pair of tongs. He was wearing an apron that looked bloodstained.

"Rex, meet my husband, Harry," Evangeline said.

He came over and shook my hand.

"You're the new neighbour."

"I am."

"Excuse the blood stained butcher's apron, one of my wife's jokes."

"I think it suits him," Evangeline said, handing me a glass of champagne.

I heard a splash as someone got into the pool. Its water was an intense blue, and I looked away from it into Evangeline's emerald eyes. There was mischief and knowledge in her face, and I watched the sun on her dark hair, and on her shoulders that day of the first of her many summer parties.

"How you settling in?" Harry said, picking up his tongs.

"Not bad. Unpacking's always a chore."

"I hear you're living there alone."

"Just a quiet neighbour," I said.

"No kids?"

I shook my head.

He was looking over my shoulder and I followed his line of vision as it tracked Evangeline around the pool. She was laughing with the man in the shorts and at one point she put her hand on his chest, to avoid spilling her drink.

"Something's funny," I said.

"Looks like it."

Harry went to put more steaks on the barbecue and I found myself shaking hands with the fat man.

"Kevin," he said, pumping my hand, "Kevin Fancy."

"Rex."

"I don't think I've ever seen you at one of the Glass parties before. They're quite a hoot, especially when the women get drunk and plunge in."

He performed a diving motion that made him look like a walrus.

"I just moved in next door."

"Oh, you're the new neighbour. I don't live in Broadlands Avenue, but I'm a Shepperton boy, have been for years. This is my wife, Samantha."

As we were talking, I'd seen one of the lounging women get up, slip into a skirt, and walk over with a wine glass in her hand. She was in her late thirties,

dark skinned, and looked like she'd peroxided her hair until most of the nu-
trients had been stripped out of it. But she was attractive in a brash way. She
had full lips and dissatisfaction written into the lines on her face. Her hand was
cool and she left it in mine just a little longer than was necessary.

"Rex," I said.

"Oh, *that* Rex, Evangeline mentioned you. You bought the end house."

"Clever chap," Kevin said, "it means he only has one neighbour. Still, with
one as charming as Evangeline, who needs more? Another G & T, Samantha?"

She nodded.

"How do you like The Telescope?" she said.

"It's perfect for what I want."

"And what's that?"

"Privacy."

"Are you a bachelor?"

"You could say that."

Her eyes wandered to Evangeline, who was talking to Kevin. As Samantha
stood there in a purple bikini top, polka dots dancing across her large breasts,
she seemed to be weighing her hostess up. I felt the crackle of hostility hover
in the air around azure blue, ever cool, Evangeline.

The party began to fill out. Couples arrived every few minutes until there
was almost no room to maoneuvre the edge of the pool. Harry watched his
wife with possessive scrutiny.

The balding guy in the shorts talked to me about property and how he was
about to pull off a major deal.

"Retirement cash," he said, in a whisper.

"Is it a secret?"

"It is from my wife, if she finds out she'll go on another shopping spree."

He punched me on the shoulder and let out a laugh that sounded like a pistol
shot.

"Did I hear my name mentioned?" the other lounging woman said.

She'd fallen asleep by the pool and now stood there looking hazy eyed.

"This is the Glass's new neighbour," he said.

"Oh, Brad, you simply are dreadful with names."

He put his hand to his mouth. The gesture made him look like a bizarre
manikin.

"Rex," I said.

His wife shook my hand.

"Alberta."

She was pink faced from the sun and her fair eyelashes made her small eyes look empty of expression.

"These parties have something of a reputation," Brad said.

Alberta put her hand on my arm.

"Oh yes, all sorts of naughty things happen, haven't you heard about the Shepperton orgies?"

I mustered a laugh as Evangeline joined us.

"Are you gossiping about me?" she said.

Alberta attempted a sly smile that made her look feckless. It didn't suit her flat face.

"Of course," she said.

Evangeline took me by the arm.

"Now, Rex, I want you to meet everyone, I can't have the Smythes hogging you."

I spoke to most of them, the tired wives and loud husbands, and thought about my new house, empty of the pretensions that were beginning to grate on me. They were not Evangeline's, but those of her strange array of guests, all uncomfortable, all trying just a little too hard. But then everyone looked awkward in Evangeline's presence.

I found Harry annoying and aggressive, and wondered briefly what I was doing there that Saturday as the sky held the promise of a hotter day in its blue canopy. And I saw the answer as she stood by the pool and removed her sarong. It was a simple, sensual gesture that almost stopped my heart. She arched her wrist and pulled on the tie, letting the azure silk slide down her legs. She stepped into the water in an indigo bikini. She was perfectly toned, with a model's figure, and I was aware of Harry standing next to me watching as she swam while night fell and the sky filled with stars.

Evangeline was an exotic misfit among the mundane. Samantha joined her, and a few of the other wives splashed about. They looked ungainly and awkward, like women learning to swim in middle age, while Evangeline moved as if she was in her own element and water was made for her. As she climbed the steps and dried herself with a towel, there was a moment when she caught my eye with a knowingness that chilled me. I sensed conspiracy amid the drunken chatter.

As I stood there Harry slapped me on the back.

"I made my money from scrap metal," he said, "worked my way up, now I own half of London. You could say I'm a diamond in the rough, not good enough for a lot of the people around here. What do I care? Look at what I've got. A gem, isn't she? Imagine how good looking our kids would be if we had them, but Evangeline doesn't want to mess up her figure. Who can blame her?"

We looked at her in mutual admiration, and I was aware of the warning as he squeezed my shoulder.

"Coming for a swim?" he said, removing his apron.

His chest was covered in a large tattoo of a snake and his right arm sported the letter E.

"No thanks."

He paused on the pool steps.

"What is it you do, Rex?"

"I'm retired."

He began to swim, his head floating in the spotlight, a black helmet of menace covering his submerged body.

I was putting my glass down on a poolside table when Samantha came up to me and said, "You mustn't take any notice of Harry, he's jealous, that's all."

"He's no need to be where I'm concerned."

"Still, I can't blame him. Evangeline's a friend, but sometimes…"

I waited for her to finish.

"Sometimes?" I said.

"She pushes things too far."

3.

She rang the bell a week later. I'd got most of the things I wanted out of the boxes and placed them where I felt they belonged. It was a precarious exercise, since many of them didn't seem to fit anywhere in the new house. I put the only two pictures that I'd packed in the living room, side by side on the recess next to the French doors. I spent one frustrating afternoon moving some vases from room to room, eventually deciding to give them to a charity shop. Vases without flowers always brought to mind images of sterility, vast metal corridors empty of people.

I'd just finished lunch when I opened the door to see Evangeline standing there in a satin red pencil skirt and matching sequin halter top. She lifted her Chanel sunglasses and tucked them into her brunette hair.

"Are you unpacked, Rex?"

"More or less."

"I thought I'd see if you needed a hand."

"You any good with a corkscrew?"

She put her palm out and I led her into the cool hall.

"It really is a beautiful house," she said. "If I didn't love mine so much I'd buy it off you."

"Too much space?"

"Not enough. Now what I want to know is why a bachelor needs all these rooms."

"You can never have too many," I said, passing her the last of the 1978 Montrachet.

"Very nice," she said, as she pulled the cork.

I poured us a glass each and we wandered through The Telescope. Evangeline stopped every so often to take in a detail.

In the living room she picked up one of the pictures.

"She's pretty," she said. "Such pale skin, and beautiful eyes. I'm sorry, how nosy of me."

She put it down.

We sat outside and looked at the garden as we finished our wine.

"I enjoyed the party," I said.

"Good, because there will be more of them and a sure way to keep the new neighbour friendly is to invite him to them. And next time I want you to swim. Everyone's asking about you."

"I can't see why I'm of such interest."

"Rex, you're a single man living alone in this huge place."

"I see, they think I have a story. They'll be disappointed when they find out how uninteresting I am."

"Everyone has a story, Rex. This place was seen by several families with children before you stole it from them with a full cash offer. The agent's a friend of ours. People wonder why you need such a big place. They're not being nosy, it's just the way they are round here. Harry hated it when we arrived. I told him we should throw parties. That way you can let the neighbours know what you want them to about your life. You see, it's the fact you have no kids that makes them curious."

"I did."

"Did?"

"You saw her, in the living room."

She put her hand on my arm.

"I'm so sorry. I feel awful."

"I can't talk about it."

"I understand, Rex. We can't have kids."

I thought for a moment she was talking about us, then I remembered she was married.

I watched through the window as she walked down the drive. The pane of glass reminded me of a lens.

A bubble of pain was swelling inside me, as somewhere outside a radio played Beyonce's Diva. All afternoon I heard the repetitive sound of camera shutters.

4.

I was missing the Montrachet and ordered several more cases of it as well as some Premier Cru Meursault from Berry Bros in London. They arrived the next day as I noted the Macallan was running out. I set them twelve at a time on the quartz counter and looked at the liquid behind the glass, clear, unmarked, reassuring it its captive purity.

I was placing them in the fridge when I heard Evangeline's voice coming from next door, and I walked into the garden to listen. She was talking on her mobile.

"I know I said two but I can't make it, something's come up, you know how it is with Harry, how he gets. No, he hasn't done anything to me, but I can't call you on this phone, he's been looking at the bills... OK I'll see you then."

She was the other side of the high fence, barely a few feet from me, and I could smell her perfume. The vanilla and musk hovered in the hot air. Unmistakeable. She was wearing Shalini. My garden suddenly felt erotic as I stood in its green, well tended enclosure listening to her.

I heard the clack of her heels on the stone patio and the sliding of doors. Her odour left me itching for a drop of whisky.

I waited until lunch, when I had some crab and salad and two shots of my diminishing solace, liquid gold in the glass.

I hadn't showered and I went upstairs, where the running water made me crave more drink.

I can say now I hadn't planned it. But that day the sound started again. It was as familiar as an itch. It wouldn't stop. It was like a million cameras on a photo shoot. It was incessant, nagging, and I knew it wouldn't let up until I'd made the purchase and stood at my customary position, one step away from the world.

That afternoon I ordered the Red One Mysterium X cinema camera. It shot at 4k resolution and would provide the kind of quality I needed.

* * *

They had another party that evening. Evangeline rang the door bell but I ignored her. I sat at the back of The Telescope and finished the Macellan. I listened to the laughter rising in the summer air. The sky was an intense blue as the moon came up and I heard the sound of splashing from the swimming pool.

Then I went inside and made sure every tap in my house was shut tight. I lay in the dark hearing their voices.

THE WORLD NEXT DOOR

5.

The Mysterium X arrived the following week. I unpacked it slowly in the living room as temperatures broke all records. My house felt like a film studio. I could hear the murmur actors and actresses learning their parts, as a secret script unfurled in my brain.

It was a professional camera, and its lens renewed the world for me. I entered its visual reality, breathless, alone, as I scanned images into my head.

As I was filming, another package arrived, a Glenfarclas 1955. I sipped two fingers as I enjoyed the Mysterium. The whisky was exceptional, not quite the standard of the Macellan, but noticeably distinguished. A silky taste lingered in its fire. It made me think of the rustle of Evangeline's silk skirt, the material swishing as she entered The Telescope, assured and composed, an unmined emerald in flesh. And I thought how Evangeline unrecorded was beauty wasted, and each fragment of time that passed without the details of her face and movement of her body being captured was a loss. I would record her on the machine of memory I held in my hand.

I began on the house. I took shots of the garden, the lawns and fountain, and the camera lived up to its name. As I was closing the French doors the bell rang. I fully expected to see Evangeline standing there. Instead I was faced with the estate agent I bought The Telescope from.

"Hello, Mr. Allen, I hope you're enjoying the house?"

"I am."

I stood there with my hand on the door and no intention of letting him in. He reminded me of something unpleasant from the past that I couldn't define.

"Enough to sell it?"

"I'm sorry?"

"I couldn't get through on your mobile."

"You have my old number."

"I see. I have a client who is prepared to make a cash offer, which would be a huge profit on the money you paid."

"Thank you for letting me know, but I'm not interested in selling."

"Would you like me to send you the paperwork?"

"I'm never selling this place," I said, and closed the door.

I had everything I needed there. I had the world, even though its shape was lost to me.

I watched the film and was pleased with the quality. I went into the bathroom and inspected my face in the mirror. My features were too defined, and so I examined them through the lens of the X, comforted by the optical distance and altered focus.

6.

She came over the next day wearing an emerald green sleeveless top and shorts.

"Join us tonight Rex, we've got too much booze, it's only a few of us."

"Glass of wine?"

I had to invite her in, I couldn't leave a woman like Evangeline on the threshold.

As we sat outside I felt she was watching me. A form of observation already existed between us.

"You do stock a good cellar, Rex," she said.

It was in that moment when she raised the glass to her lips that I knew what I would do. Even she was unaware of how much style she had. It was totally unrehearsed. And my fingers itched for the camera. She saw me looking at her, and paused.

I needed to tell her.

"You know, forgive me for saying so, Evangeline, but your features."

"Yes?"

"You could have been a star."

"Forgive you?"

She laughed and reached into her bag. I watched as she lit an Epique Superslim.

"Unusual choice of cigarette," I said.

"I have unusual tastes, Rex."

I drank some Montrachet as smoke filled the air and she tipped her face skyward, blowing a plume towards heaven. But it was her lighter that brought the noise of camera shutters into my head. It was chrome, and the flash it produced in the bright sunlight as she put it back in her bag left me hungry and alone.

"I did want to act," she said.

"You would look good on film."

"Then Harry bought me."

"You're not too old," I said.

"I'm 32."

"Would Harry disapprove?"

She didn't answer, and I watched a drop of water crawl down the outer bell of her glass as it nestled in her hand.

"I better go," she said, looking at her watch, "I'm meeting a friend for lunch, and I'm late."

She stood up.

"I hope I haven't said too much."

"Can I use your phone? Harry's confiscated mine."

"I don't have a phone."

"I'm only joking," she said, "I've left it somewhere and can't find it." She prodded me in the shoulder. "Now tell me where it is, Rex."

"I don't have a landline, you can use my mobile."

She followed me inside and I left her as she made the call.

From the living room I heard her say, "I know, it's frustrating, but I'll make it up to you, see you soon."

The sense of complicity deepened as she came through, kissed me on the cheek, and said, "See you tonight, Rex."

After she left I checked my phone. She'd deleted the number she called. I turned on the X. It made the noise stop.

7.

I went to the party as night stayed away from the deep blue sky and I watched Evangeline among her many guests. The crowd was much the same, with a few additions, business contacts of Harry, who'd come to make deals. Evangeline exerted her beauty softly, subtly upstaging the other wives. I wondered if she did it deliberately, and how she would behave if she had competition. But she was the star. Harry provided her with a lifestyle and I wondered how much her marriage mattered to her.

The presence of the guests was a wall between me and her. I wanted to leave and watch the world from behind the X. I wanted to copy her image a million times and trace her face in the darkness, like the lines on a map. I was pouring myself some more wine when I felt a hand on my shoulder. I turned to see Samantha standing there, looking drunk.

"Rex, good to see you again."

She held up her glass and I filled it and sat with her by the pool.

"You don't seem to be enjoying yourself," she said.

"Oh?"

"You've been standing on your own watching her all evening."

"Who?"

"I don't know what they see in her."

"Are you talking about our hostess?"

"I am Rex, I am."

"She does it well."

"What?"

"Entertain."

"Oh, she's entertaining all right, when she's not trying to steal your husband."

"Are you saying she and Kevin…?"

"No, don't be silly." Her eyes looked heavy, and her voice was slurred, as she laid her hand on my knee. "Kevin was all right in his younger days. How come you're not married, Rex?"

"It's a long story."

"This Pinot Grigio's barely cool," she said, running her finger along the edge of the glass.

"Nothing stays cold in this heat."

"Except her."

"I wouldn't say she's cold."

"Frigid."

"You think?"

"Evangeline," she said, whispering, "wants to be the only woman round here. Alberta tries to upstage her. She says silly things to draw attention to herself. Evangeline makes it clear that she thinks she's a cut above us. We're her friends all right, but we know our place."

"So what makes you keep coming?"

"I like the parties, she's never going to do anything with Kevin, but I wish she'd make it less obvious how she views herself. You better watch out, Rex, she may get you in trouble."

"I don't think Evangeline is interested in me."

"Perhaps not in the way you think, but she likes to get what she wants."

"And what does she want?"

"Everything, Rex, everything."

Just then Kevin emerged from the long shadows by the pool.

"There you are, I thought you'd fallen in," he said. "Never let her near water with a drink in her hand, Rex. Samantha, time to go."

She rose and waved at me. I sat there for a while staring at the yawning black mass of the pool. It represented something sick and defiled. Evangeline was laughing with Alberta as I stole away, along the side passage and to the quiet of The Telescope.

WATCHING EVANGELINE

8.

Obsession is not a modern disease. Its roots lie deep inside humanity and may be the reason we're here. You don't know you're obsessed until you can't move, until all you see is the one thing. By then the tendrils have wrapped themselves around your tidy heart. They're delicate at first in their unfolding, touching you in the dark, like the soft caress of a lover at dawn. Then you know they're squeezing the blood out of you, and that you will have to hack them away and with them some living beating part of yourself to be free.

I held the camera and captured her image again and again that intoxicated summer when music filled the gardens of Broadlands Avenue, and Evangeline was high forever.

Stars have a rare quality, an ability to take away the smallness most men feel. They're more corrupt than us, but the corruption is better hidden, and their appeal is a lie, the biggest drug you will ever know.

Evangeline was a complete balance of all the qualities famous stars have. She knew she was a rare flame.

All that summer I watched her. I caught her laughing, smiling, looking away from Harry, alone, contemplating her day. I took her with shopping bags on the empty drive next door, and I filmed her sunbathing by the pool, her body tanned and glowing in the unnatural sun that seemed to set that time apart. For she seemed to exist outside time. And I captured her and made her mine.

I spent my evenings with a glass of Montrachet chilling my tongue as I sipped her image from the Plasma screen in my living room. I fed on her. The X bridged the space between us. I zoomed in on her, caressing her skin with the lens. I entered her world like a hummingbird penetrating a flower, my heart beating like rapid wings. She existed in my watchfulness and awoke my desire. When I wasn't filming her, time was static. There were no clocks in The Telescope. I felt erased when I wasn't watching her image. My house had no past and no future.

I never used most of the rooms, existing in solitude, with only the films I took. And I felt more and more that I was part of a plot, and my only defence against it was the camera, as if Evangeline and Harry knew things that they were keeping from me and the X would find them out. I felt chilled, as if some lost piece of knowledge was frozen inside me. Sometimes at night as the Glenfarclas wore off I could hear icebergs breaking a long way off, and then the notes of Fleetwood Mac's "The Chain" would stab at my brain like shards of glass against a nerve.

* * *

The camera found the other woman who lived inside her. Evangeline had a range of expressions. I loved to watch her sit in the summer sun, her skin darkening, her face perfectly unlined, and see her contemplate the pool. I took her as she entered the water, the blue depths covering her body while she swam in the afternoons. At times she looked troubled, and she'd walk about the lawn with an expression I studied for many hours at night. It was a look I wanted to penetrate, and it belonged to someone else.

And the noise stopped. It stopped completely as I filmed.

I studied her movements. She had a slow way of walking when she wanted to be watched, and she would glow in the attention she received at her parties. She used her hands to good effect, emphasizing her sensuality in gestures that ranged from the way she sipped from her glass to the way she would hold her cigarette and turn away, as if there was sadness in the act. She wanted to know your eyes were on her without acknowledging you. But there was much she wasn't saying. Harry only got to see one part of her. It was almost as if he was afraid to see more. He played the role of her boastful proprietor. But I was taking pieces of her away with me.

I would film her through the window of my bathroom, or from the recess of my terrace, dressed in black, sweating on the summer nights. The camera liked her, it was drawn towards her face and body, and touched her outlines in its world. I sometimes wondered if she knew, if secretly she desired it.

It was when she was alone that I observed the most about her. I saw the things that she kept hidden, even from herself.

The X caught her voice well. It was suggestive and feminine, rich in sexual allure, like a saxophone in a smoky room. I longed for the clarity of it up close. I wanted her to speak someone else's lines, not the script that Harry had given her. She was born to play the part, I just needed to secure her time, and reel her in.

One day I saw her on her drive. She was talking on her mobile and hung up as I was leaving.

"Could you do me a favour, Evangeline?"

"Of course."

"I'm not getting any incoming calls, could you try my number?"

"What is it?"

I told her and watched it ring.

"How odd," I said.

"Seems to be working, or maybe it only responds to me."

I stored her number in my phone's memory. I was making a record of her that summer, lost as I was in the green landscape and the sweltering heat.

Each night I would lie down with her image in my mind. There was no tomorrow, only the present of Evangeline, and all she represented in her dark and violent glory.

She was made for the camera. Sometimes I thought beneath the surface of her translucent green eyes she was filming me.

9.

I traced every detail of her unblemished skin onto film. For it is in skin that beauty lives, forever. Until some fire takes it away. Then it crumples like a leaf.

I studied Evangeline's features, spending endless hours comparing them to the pictures of stars through history, young women caught in the ephemeral trap of eternalising looks.

I watched her from behind the lens, lost in the whispering melody of the camera's mechanism. It altered her, and showed her to be not a thing of flesh, but something more, something other, and I began to crave her company. I wanted to film her as she slept and yielded knowledge of the workings of her mind. One day she walked naked through the garden to the pool and I caught my breath at her body's perfection. As she left the water and dried herself she looked around momentarily, as if she was aware I was watching her.

She liked to be watched. In fulfilling her desire, I was her lover in a sense. There is a shadow lover for every woman, a secret being they seek in other men, who lies beyond touch. He is the fulfilment of all hidden desires, and a woman's nature alters at his touch. There were things Evangeline was pushing away, but the camera was capturing them. I saw her move at night on my screen, slowed down, solitary, in the images I pored over again and again, searching for clues in her gestures, as if she was a code I was sent to The Telescope to decipher. She held a key. But the lock was lost.

You see, I was the only one who understood her. None of the others did, not her husband, not her friends, who idly went to her parties. Evangeline had set herself on display and she began to show more of herself to me. Not just her body, but her soul. A real film maker captures the soul, and places it on film.

I found out her secret self. I learned the hidden Evangeline until she sat in my palm. She needed to be known. She wanted to be watched.

That was the reason for her secret visits to me, her references to Harry, her watchfulness as she sat next to me smoking on my terrace. She was inviting me in.

10.

Sometimes she told me things when she was alone. At night, as I watched that day's film, she seemed to be making small movements with her mouth. I read her lips. I read the shape of their erotic display. There are many forms of nakedness. There were things Evangeline wanted me to know. The watcher and the watched. The harness and the plough.

I avoided her parties. I filmed them instead. Sometimes at night the gurgling of water would trouble my sleep and I wandered the empty corridors of my house, checking the taps. I rarely bathed. My showers were quick and perfunctory, barely enough to wash the sweat from my skin, a sweat that belonged there since Evangeline caused it to break from my pores like wine.

Days passed when I only saw her through the lens. She belonged there.

Then, one weekend, Harry went away on business. I heard his loud voice outside that Saturday morning. I rose and stared through sleepy eyes out of the window. He put a case in the boot, kissed Evangeline on the cheek, and drove off in his Alfa Romeo. Later I heard her car on the gravel drive.

I waited for her until noon and ate some lunch. She returned late and didn't appear until the next morning when she left her house and drove away in her SLR McLaren. Harry had to show her off, even in the vehicle she drove. She was gone all day and I felt a gnawing sensation. I drank the rest of the Glenfarclas as I watched every film I had of her in my darkened living room, while outside the streets cracked in the relentless heat. I stepped into my garden as night fell and inhaled the violent odours of a summer when people lost their inhibitions and their scruples, when the world died again and I was reborn. The night was full of erotic shadows and I searched for Evangeline's among them. But the house next door was silent, the windows darkened, and I wondered where she'd gone.

She had another life, one outside my surveillance of her. I emptied the bottle and sat staring at the pictures of my dead daughter. I watched from my window for Evangeline to return. She didn't. Eventually, I fell asleep.

I was woken the next morning by the sound of her car drawing up. She got out before I could see her, and an hour later Harry returned.

I looked around my house and realised everything looked static. I took the X from room to room with me all day, waiting for a glimpse of her, but Evangeline stayed inside.

At twilight I heard raised voices over the garden wall. Harry was shouting, and I couldn't make out what was being said, but I heard Evangeline cry out, "No, no."

The next morning I saw her leave early. She glanced up and saw me watching her and I took my first shower in days.

11.

The following afternoon she rang the bell.

"We're having another party tonight, Rex," she said. "Do come."

"Oh, I don't know."

"Are you hiding from us?"

"No."

She inched towards me.

"You're not watching me, are you Rex?"

"Watching you?"

"Yesterday I saw you looking out of your window."

"Oh, that. I was waiting for a parcel to arrive."

"Bit early. Anyway, come tonight, or else."

"I'd love to."

She looked at me over the rim of her Channel sunglasses.

"I like being watched, Rex, but not in that way."

She walked away and I considered my options.

She didn't seem angry. There was invitation in her words and recognition in her eyes.

I went that evening. I spent a few hours drinking Pinot Grigio and watching Evangeline. I didn't get the chance to speak to her. Harry followed her around all night. I could hear him raise his voice as she went into the kitchen. She was wearing a halter neck top and as she stood in the light I thought I saw a bruise on her shoulder. Then she retreated into the house and came out wearing a blouse.

Her figure was a shadow compared to the images I had at home. She was less alive in her house, than in the life I was making for her. And as I talked to her guests I thought that the real Evangeline lived next door, in The Telescope. I was preparing the stage for her stardom. One day I would show her.

She was made for film. Stars are like that. They only come alive in certain skies. They need the purity of film to breathe.

12.

I had to do something, and so I bought the Nikon P510. I needed to watch her other life. I couldn't let the film stop running. I couldn't live with fractured images.

Its zoom capacity was outstanding for its size. I stared at it with resignation, settling for the still picture, until I restored the moving body.

I hired a black Ford Kuga. I parked it at the end of Broadlands Avenue and waited.

All through that slow day of building heat I watched the front of her house from the end of the avenue. I sat in the air conditioned Ford with the Nikon on the seat, while outside the temperature reached 106 degrees.

Eventually she left and got in her car. I followed her out of Shepperton and to Richmond, where she pulled up outside a Victorian house. I resented being brought back there to the past.

I watched her get a ticket from a parking machine. She was wearing a violet pencil skirt and floral blouse. She buzzed and went inside. From the number of bells on the front door I could see the house was divided into flats.

I waited for an hour. When she emerged she was with a blonde tanned man. He had an athletic build and a fire about him. They passed me and at the end of the road he kissed her. It lasted long enough for me to take a few shots from the stillness of the car. I studied the pictures.

There was an intimacy between Evangeline and this stranger that indicated a history. It was one I was unaware of and in that moment the films at my house seemed full of holes. The reality they afforded me was suddenly in question.

I waited.

I had no jealousy towards her lover. What I needed from Evangeline was neither moral purity nor fidelity, but some cohesion that this stranger's presence interrupted. I considered how much I knew about her. Seeing corruption in her character was pleasing. The camera was finding all the hidden things in her.

After a few hours they returned. She kissed him in the street. Then she got in her car and drove away.

I watched him go inside. He looked like a gigolo.

I drove back slowly and parked the Ford at the end of the Avenue, walking into my house with the camera under my arm.

I sat and watched the films as a party started next door.

The images seemed empty and I felt tricked.

I wondered if she'd been putting on a show. Perhaps she'd invited me to watch her, knowing all along that I didn't guess her secret. Perhaps that was the nature of her lie. I knew then that I had to remove any deceit that lay between us. Her lover may penetrate her body, but I would penetrate her soul.

From my terrace I shot her below with her guests. She was wearing an off shoulder party dress. I could see no bruise on her skin. I imagined the man I'd seen that afternoon touching her.

But Evangeline looked empty now and that night I studied the film I'd taken, as her guests left and silence descended on the Avenue. The static shots from the Nikon showed some part of her the film had missed. And I realised she'd been acting all along, among her guests and with Harry. I wanted to film her in the right context. I needed some singular form of privacy in which to reveal Evangeline.

She could have a hundred lovers. I didn't want her body. I wanted something else entirely from her than the thing she gave to other men.

13.

I watched her with Michael Flame. I found out his name without too much difficulty. Evangeline always rang the bell to flat number 2. As they went out one day I sat in the Ford and saw the postman deliver his mail. He left some sticking out of the letterbox. A quick glance gave me the information I wanted and I removed his phone bill.

It detailed his calls, and I recognised Evangeline's mobile number on there. As I added up the hours they spent talking to one another I estimated how long her affair had been going on.

They returned some time later and went into his flat. When she left she had that glow on her face she carried to her parties. But there was something else in her expression, something the Nikon captured. She wore a look of deep sexual exultation. It was a look I had never seen in her before. It would fade by the time she reached her house. The sense of pleasure she took from her meetings with her lover heightened her appeal among her guests. There seemed to be little pleasure between her and Harry. If he was bruising Evangeline, her affair was removing the marks. Suddenly she seemed fragile, and I wanted to find out more.

Michael Flame made a lot of calls. I dialled them all, withholding my number on a cheap pay as you go mobile. Most of them were to women and I concluded he was conducting a number of affairs. I wondered if Evangeline knew.

She needed to be the only one. Stars are like that.

I spent hours following her to her meetings with Michael. I watched her embrace him and laugh, I watched her return to Harry and heard them argue.

I pored over the films, observing the difference between the way she was at home, and the way she was with Michael.

Next door she was on show and Harry had put her there. I knew this and what it entailed. I knew all about Evangeline.

14.

She invited it, of course, the watchfulness. She needed it, for without the attention Evangeline felt she didn't exist. She wanted to know when she was being watched and that is the problem with stars. They want to control the camera.

I'd accumulated over twenty-four hours of film when she visited Michael one day. I'd bought a through wall listening device that could pick up conversations from a distance and I honed in on his flat as they went inside.

It was still in the hundreds and his window overlooking the street was open. I saw him standing next to it as I began recording.

I heard them alone.

I heard Evangeline gasp with pleasure. I heard her moan.

I sat there in the Ford with images running in my mind. And for the first time I felt angry.

The quality of the recording was good. But I couldn't film her. It wasn't that I wanted to film her having sex, I wanted to capture every part of her on camera.

As I was leaving she came out into the street. I drove past her and she saw me and stood staring after me as I turned the corner.

I waited for her call. It never came.

I listened to the sounds of her sexual pleasure. I considered what it told me about her as a woman.

And I knew what she was. I'd known it all along, from the first moment I saw her and she invited me over.

15.

She came round the next day.

"Rex, we need to talk."

I showed her through to the living room.

"Can I offer you a glass of wine?"

"I haven't come here for a drink. I saw you yesterday, you've been following me."

"I have."

"Why?"

"Does it matter, Evangeline?"

"Of course it matters."

"So you have a lover."

"You are presumptuous."

"Am I?"

There was someone else inside her, someone she didn't know, and I had to have her. I could see her sliding around beneath her skin, I could hear her voice in the sexual moans I had on tape. I felt the key turning in the lock, and I tried the handle of the door.

"I have something to show you," I said.

There are moments when we act out of character. I did then, in coercing her into a position whose precise geography I understood no more than I did myself.

I put on one of the films. I watched her face drop in disbelief as she saw herself at home, on the phone, walking about her garden, entertaining guests.

"What kind of sick voyeur are you?" she said.

"I'm making films, Evangeline. I don't mind if you're having an affair."

"Affair? All you've got there is me in my garden. But this is an invasion of my privacy."

"You don't have any privacy, women like you never do. Why do you think stars commit suicide?"

As she raised her arms I thought she was going to hit me. Instead she crossed them and stood staring at me.

I played her the recording and showed her the shots of her and Michael.

"So you're blackmailing me. Why Rex, what did I ever do to you?"

"I'm not blackmailing you, I don't need your money."

"What then?"

"I understand you far more than you realise."

"I invite you to my parties, you stay away, and you do this."

"Your affair can continue."

"What do you want?"

"I want to show you who you are."

"This is insanity."

"I know things about you."

"Yes, because you've been spying on me."

I had to have her. I had to finish the film. I would never have told Harry. But her belief that I would was the only key I had. She was already mine, and I knew it.

"I won't tell Harry on one condition," I said.

"You want to have sex with me?"

"I want you to play a part."

"What part?"

"I want you to play Coral."

"And who's Coral?"

"You'll find out. I want you to meet me once a week for two hours. I will tell you what to wear."

The look she gave me then will never leave me.

"There's no sex involved?"

"No."

"That's all you want, Rex?"

"I'll cover for you if Harry suspects your affair with Michael."

"You even know his name."

"I can be your alibi."

"I need to think about this, I need to know more about what I'm getting involved in."

I watched her walk down my drive. I knew which dress she would wear for the first time.

16.

I didn't see Evangeline the next day. There was no party. The house next door lay in a hush, the windows closed. I noticed when I went out, that both cars were gone from the drive. I wondered if she and Harry had taken off somewhere to repair their broken marriage. I considered how much honesty lay between them and concluded none. Evangeline was his show thing. He would never accept another man having her. Watching was allowed, but no more. I knew that was why I was on safe territory with her. She was already acting a part for him, she was already trapped. Her private time with Michael was what interested me. I wanted to find the other Evangeline.

And I wondered who Coral was and why I'd mentioned her name. It was as familiar as the shapeless bruise of grief in my sleeping heart. I felt disconnected from my words. My deeds seemed compulsions, rather than choices.

I sat in my living room and looked at the pictures from my past. My daughter's face was set in sepia, a relic of someone else's life. I looked at myself in the bathroom mirror, my eyes like camera lenses beneath the polished Gucci metal frames. I watched the films, the endless hours of Evangeline alone, unaware she was being filmed.

The following day I saw her. She was on the drive and when I came out she stood still, watching me. Away from the X she was not the woman I'd captured. I knew the reality of her, the film had shown me, I just needed to introduce her to herself.

"Does next Tuesday suit?" I said.

"What time?"

"Two o'clock."

"I'll do what I can."

"Can you wear the floral print skirt and matching blouse?"
She frowned with indignation.
I saw no hatred in her eyes.
"OK Rex, just don't push this too far."

PLAYING CORAL

17.

She was a few minutes late. I was drinking chilled Premier Cru Meursault when she rang the bell. Her glass stood waiting on the quartz counter. I knew she'd come. They always do. Stars.

She was wearing the outfit, the first one I'd seen her in those hot weeks ago when she first called to me on my drive.

I knew how much cooperation existed in her soul, it was a still and sleeping aspect of her being at enmity with who she pretended to be. That is partly why she agreed to it, I knew how pliable she was.

She followed me through to the kitchen where I filled her glass.

"I want to make one thing clear," she said, "I don't like this, I'm only doing it because you're blackmailing me."

"This isn't blackmail."

"There's no money involved, but you're holding me to ransom. I don't want Harry finding out. I want my marriage, Rex. I don't know how much you think you know about it, but you don't understand what Harry gives me, and I don't want it taken away."

"I only want you to play Coral."

"Who is she?"

"I don't know."

"Some ex who jilted you?"

"That's a tired old plot, I want a new film."

"You're a voyeur. Have you filmed me getting fucked?"

"No."

"How can I play Coral if I don't know who she is?"

"You'll find her."

"Where?"

"Inside yourself."

"What is it you want to know about me?"

"Let's eat."

"Eat!"

She followed me through to the dining room where I pulled her chair back and watched her sit down. She looked just like her and my memory began to ache.

I wanted to satisfy her tastes. I'd studied her habits and bought the things she enjoyed. I looked for pleasure in her face. But I wanted far more in return.

We ate wild Alaskan salmon and salads. I looked at her translucent green eyes. I watched her mannerisms, taking note as the spy camera filmed her.

I'd positioned it on the dresser. I would tell her about it later. I wanted her to be natural when the real filming began.

And as she moved, there seemed to be two women there, the other revealing herself in the interludes between her gestures. Sometimes her eyes changed shade, to a different hue of green. She knew what I'd lost, she would be my memory.

"You want to meet me once a week and have me play a part?" she said.

"Yes."

"How can I do that when you won't tell me who she is?"

"We will discover who Coral is, you will help me."

"Rex, I think you're troubled."

Afterwards I showed her the catalogue.

"I've picked some clothes out for you."

"You're going to dress me up now, are you?"

"I need things to be arranged a certain way so you can be Coral."

"I don't like being told what to wear."

"Harry controls you."

"Harry lets me get away with quite a lot."

"But not Michael."

"Don't pretend to understand me."

But I did understand her. I knew that Harry gave her status, and how valuable that was to her.

She looked at the catalogue, turning the glossy pages with sharp fingernails.

"I wouldn't wear a lot of these," she said.

44

"No one else will see you in them."

"Just you."

"That's right."

"Are you going to watch me getting dressed in them, is that it Rex?"

"No. Come here wearing what you want, you can go upstairs and dress, then join me for lunch or dinner if you can get away from Harry in the evenings."

"You know, I liked you Rex."

"You will again, Evangeline."

She put the catalogue down.

"Why do you want me to do this?"

"Are you saying you're not already acting?"

"I'll let you decide what you want me to wear, that way I can find out who she is."

"You make her sound like a rival," I said.

"Either you know who Coral is or you don't."

"I know her like a melody without the words, and the words are hidden somewhere inside you."

She left at four o'clock. I watched the film I'd taken that day. It wasn't bad quality, but lacked the angles necessary for what I wanted to do. I noticed Evangeline relax a little during lunch and that pleased me. She would relax more. She would make a perfect Coral. The things we know most deeply are not conscious.

I heard another party next door that evening. I was not invited. I never wanted to attend her parties, another guest there to watch her among the crowd. I wanted a privileged seat. I wanted to see her in those rare, intimate moments that not even Harry shared with her. Those were the moments that would make her into a star. I picked the outfit for her next visit. It would show Evangeline's figure perfectly.

18.

The following Tuesday she came at 2 o'clock. I'd placed the blue Fendi dress on a chair in one of the spare rooms. It lay there like a piece of the sky, and I wanted to see it touch her skin. She walked into the hall, looked around, and said, "So, this is when you want me to dress up."

I showed her upstairs and left her while I poured some wine, a new delivery of Les Culs de Beaujeu Sancerre I'd chilled to exactly the right temperature. It was some time before she reappeared. I considered whether she would begin to rebel against the part, but a star always knows when a role suits her.

When she entered the kitchen I was no longer in that house in Shepperton, but somewhere else, and I stood there looking at her as she picked up her glass.

"So, Rex, what do you have planned for today?"

"Lunch and two hours of you as Coral."

"You know as I walked here this felt like an affair. Harry's at work, and you've leased this slice of me, my time."

"We're not having an affair, Evangeline."

"You're compromising me."

She enjoyed the lunch. I'd cooked the finest beef and sliced it thin and pink. She sipped her wine with that sensuous movement of hers, as if she was kissing the lip of the glass. Her mouth had this extraordinary sexual quality I have never seen in another woman. She stared through the windows at my garden, as if she existed there beyond the part she would act so well. She looked as though she was playing to the camera, which lay secreted to her side, and I considered whether she knew all along and it was me who was being coerced by her into the drama that began to unfold.

She drank too much.

"You know, when I used to see Michael, I never felt this way. I'd meet him, return to Harry, and wash his smell from my body. But I can't wash this away."

"We're not having sex, Evangeline."

"Maybe it's because it's next door. When I look out of my window and see your house it's a guilty secret for me to drag around my home, thinking of what you know about me and the threat to tell Harry."

"I never threatened to tell Harry."

"You implied it."

"I said I'd cover for you."

"I know men, Rex, and I've been trying to figure you out. You're a voyeur, do you want to film me being screwed?"

I smiled at her.

"You can still see Michael."

"Can I? Thank you. How nice of you. What else can I do?"

"I don't want you to change your life, Evangeline, just to be mine for two hours a week."

"Why?"

"Because you can play Coral."

"Who is she, Rex?"

"That's what we'll find out."

"If I let you fuck me would that be it? Would it be enough?"

"That is not what I want."

"Don't get me wrong, I'm not offering to sleep with you. Having me act this part is weirder."

"If we had sex, you'd feel more in control, Evangeline, that's all."

"So how do I play her, Rex?"

"Be a star, dress in the clothes I give you and discover her."

She stood up and walked over to me. She laid a warm hand on my shoulder and seemed to be trying to penetrate me with her green eyes.

"It's as if you want me to pour out some hidden content of my being. You need to tell me about her, Rex, tell me about Coral."

"She is beautiful, sensual, men desire her, and she exploits her beauty to get what she wants."

For a moment I thought she saw the camera. She turned and looked at the dresser, then walked to the window.

"And what does she want, Rex?"

"Everything, Evangeline."

"I see her as corrupt."

"She may well be."

"Because you're corrupting me by doing this, that is what this is about. It's like you want me to be aware of sin."

"You're already aware of sin when you see Michael."

"It's just an affair, Rex, a simple matter, unlike this. I leave him behind when I return to Harry."

"I've seen you at your parties, Evangeline, you're playing a role."

"No, that's what you want me to do."

"You're the Evangeline that Harry wants, but what about the other one?"

"There isn't another one. You're talking about that bitch Coral."

As she invented her, so she found her. I knew she'd fit the part.

She left at four. I let her keep the outfit. I watched her walk to her house, the dress caressing her hips.

I planned the next session. I selected her clothes. Each item of the wardrobe I chose reflected a different part of Coral. It was as if she lay beyond reach, a fragment lost in time. I thought about Evangeline and Michael. The name Francis Merit entered my mind at midnight and I lay awake asking myself who he was.

19.

Whatever value we possess as human beings may be lost to us. It is as if we exist in personal blind spots. I sought Coral, as if I was diving for myself. She lay lodged inside me like an irrefutable and unknowable fact. And I knew that she lived inside Evangeline.

I saw little of Harry in those days. I didn't want to. It wasn't that I was jealous of the reminder he represented that Evangeline was someone else's wife. He was superfluous to the drama, an extra without lines.

One incident, in particular, showed me Harry.

I was coming home one day and he was on his drive sporting a bright red pair of shorts and a Miami shirt that was open at the front. His tattoo showed like a stain on his skin.

"Join me for a beer, Rex," he said.

I wanted to make an excuse, but felt it necessary to please him. My guilty relationship with his wife necessitated that.

"Thanks, I think I will, just give me a minute," I said, pointing to my shopping.

I went inside and put the groceries in my spotless fridge, inhaling the cold air as if it was a narcotic. My house was unmarked, and at times its sterility felt like an antidote to the world outside. The tins of caviar and cuts of salmon looked clinical and erotic. The fact that only my hands would open them was arousing. I thought of coaxing an oyster from its shell, the wet met giving way. I thought of Evangeline, and how I was removing that bruised piece from her.

The front door was open next door. I wandered through the downstairs and noted how, although Evangeline was the hostess who dominated the parties, it was Harry's house. The living room was comfortable and full of pictures of them. In each one Harry either had his hand on her shoulder or his arm around her waist, and he was often looking down at her, as if she was his property. But it was the other ornaments that set the tone of the home. A glass fronted cabinet showed off the golfing prizes he'd won. Lines of boxing trophies dominated the room.

As I stood there I heard footsteps. I turned round to see Harry.

"Won them all, Rex," he said. "I used to box, no one ever puts me on the canvas."

"Sorry for the intrusion, I couldn't find you."

"Come outside and feast your eyes."

I followed him through into the bright sunlight.

He was a few feet ahead of me, and the first thing I saw was Evangeline. She was sunbathing on a lounger, and she looked almost unreal. It was as if she didn't belong there, but next door at The Telescope, and this woman was a duplicate.

I don't know why I hadn't noticed them before, but I became aware of Harry's CCTV cameras trained on the swimming pool.

"Great body," he said, as if he was talking about a car.

I said nothing. Evangeline was not a body.

As Harry went inside to fetch the beers she rose.

"I didn't expect to see you here," she said.

She was full of the awkwardness of an adulteress in the dual presence of her husband and lover.

"This must make you feel as though you have to change roles."

"Roles?"

"The one you play for Harry, and the one you play for me. Which is more real?"

Harry came out with two Heinekens. I drank mine as fast as I could without making it obvious I wanted to leave. He showed no curiosity about what I might have said to Evangeline. She was his wife, and he was the proud owner of her. Harry was lost if he couldn't show her off. And inasmuch as he placed her on display, the truth of her lay hidden.

And she knew how much of herself to show. I wanted to see the rest.

I left shortly afterwards, and thought about Harry.

He didn't understand Evangeline. She existed for him merely as part of the spectacle of his days, and endless parties.

That night I heard raised voices from next door. I went onto my terrace and it fell quiet.

Then I heard Harry say, "Come on, no one's watching."

"OK, but I'll pick the spot," Evangeline said.

I watched it through the X.

They walked out, naked, past the pool to the loungers. Evangeline sat on a table and Harry entered her.

She was silent against his noise.

And as I filmed him between her thighs, Evangeline looked over his shoulder, her gaze directed at my terrace.

She had something in her hand, I didn't see what it was until Harry wandered off. Then I watched her stand ad wipe herself with one of the napkins I'd laid for our last lunch before she walked back into her house.

* * *

Once a week that torrid summer she came to my house. The times varied, and so did the days, but she always arrived punctually wearing a new outfit. She relaxed. Her initial resentments left her. I began to show her who she was.

She kept all the costumes. Sometimes she wore them at one her parties, as if she was becoming Coral.

One evening she met me while Harry was away on business. We dined by candlelight on my terrace as night fell.

She was wearing a blue pencil skirt and blouse and she looked tanned and radiant as she sipped cold wine. I could feel the heat from her skin.

"Rex, you buy me clothes and entertain me. It's as if you want me to be your woman except for the sex."

"I want you to be Coral."

"That makes me feel undesired."

"You know you're desired, Evangeline."

"Except by you."

"Not entirely, but not in the way you expect."

"You want me to act out a part for you. Some women do that in bed."

"Is that what Harry wants?"

"You've seen what Harry wants. He wants me to be his whore. He began that game the first time we made love. He likes me to dress beautifully, flirt at the parties, knowing he owns me."

"Does he?"

"No. That's why I fuck Michael."

"What does he give you?"

"Romance."

"The fact that he's younger?"

"Perhaps."

"I'll make sure you remain the age you are, Evangeline."

She shivered in the hot night air.

"I feel you're capturing me," she said.

I was, on film, as she was to find out.

20.

She shimmered in the heat. She changed as I observed her. She told me things. She told me them to shock me, jolt me out of my customary position of observer. And she revealed herself in doing so. Slowly, Evangeline was creating an intimacy with me that served as a stage on which Coral would perform.

I held her there, pinioned by her performance. Coral was coming alive, day by day, hour by expectant hour, as time crawled across the week towards each encounter, pregnant with desire and broken memory. She was a compass point in my torn life as I hunted for myself. I lived in the anticipation of her. And she gave me what I wanted.

Directing Evangeline was more intimate than sex. The camera caught her soul. A star is naked on screen, immortalised and captured. Her life is no longer hers. She belongs to the viewers, the endless set of eyes which feast on her beauty in eternity.

Evangeline gave me herself. She needed to, she needed stardom. They all surrender in the end. She began to understand who Coral was, piece by piece in those long afternoons and evenings of stolen time when we were alone together. We were tethered to the past and I was mastless there in Broadlands Avenue, lost in discovery. At times I could hear someone dragging a chain across the ground, link by staccato shackling link.

She met me one evening dressed in a short black skirt and halter top. I'd picked out some earrings for her, and the pearls set off her lobes immaculately. She had a fine profile, her ears were sensual and graceful. She seemed forever fertile, existing on the edge of an eternally alluring female fecundity.

If Evangeline had a distinctive smell, it was the odour of desire.

"Rex, is Coral an ideal?" she said.

"No, Evangeline she is corruption."

I surprised myself with the things I knew, they broke through the mist like jagged rocks. But Evangeline allowed me to know them. She replaced the mirrors in The Telescope. She showed me what I needed to know.

My life at The Telescope had seemed less than real. Events occurred in a haze, and I retreated behind the lens. But as I met with Evangeline, the world came into focus. She brought a definition with her that allowed me to remember.

I watched her lift a piece of lamb with her fork and chew slowly, her lips moist, her erotic mouth closed. She gave a new meaning to flesh with her every movement.

"What appeal does she have then?" she said.

"Her looks disguise her corruption, she is provocatively sexual. Her face is naked, as if it's some intimate part of her body."

"She is desired."

"She is constantly attended to by the eyes of men."

"I know what that feels like. I know how many of Harry's colleagues want me. Sometimes they touch me when he isn't looking. You know, a casual, seemingly innocent gesture, the hand on the shoulder that lingers a little too long, their fingers on my waist as they pass by. I ignore them, they will never have me. But sometimes I imagine their hands touching me in the dark as Harry lies next to me asleep, unable to watch me. It's as if his need to put me on display invites betrayal. I can feel you touching me in the dark sometimes, Rex. I can feel your hunger."

"How do you see Coral?"

"I see her as beautiful, and sexual. She likes to sleep with men, but needs to control them with her body, and she judges much by the body, it is all she has."

"Do you know what songs Coral likes to hear?"

"Something that denies what she wants."

"And what is it she wants?"

"To be wanted."

She knew the part through and through. It was amazing watching her change as she wore the clothes, until she was her, almost.

I wondered if she could become her entirely.

That evening as we drank wine on my terrace the sky was stained blue.

"I hated Harry when I met him," she said.

"Why did you marry him?"

"People carry diseases, Rex. We offset one another's malaise. He needed me and offered me the lifestyle I want. My hatred for him was an impression, that's all, he was showing off. Then I realised that he would give me the attention I need. Harry shows off now about business, but he lets me have what I want."

"Except a lover."

"He often says when he touches me that only his hands get to feel my skin. I have the softest skin, Rex, like silk."

She stood up and walked over to me. I was setting my glass down on the table and she took my hand and ran it along her arm.

"Can you imagine what I feel like in bed?"

"What is it you want that Harry gives to you?"

"The feeling that he couldn't exist without me."

"Do you believe that?"

"Rex, my marriage is important to me. Don't pretend to understand it."

"You hide from Harry."

"I'm hiding here with you."

"You like the attention."

"Oh, you know me, do you?"

"I know stars, Evangeline."

"You're like some pornographic astronomer here in The Telescope. You don't know me, you've cornered me into this charade and I'm getting tired of it."

"How do you feel when you leave Michael?"

"Fucked."

"Do you feel more alive or more empty?"

"Michael knows exactly how to screw me, his hands touch me in ways Harry would never dream of."

"Because Harry wants something from you and Michael is giving to you? He is young and wants you, waits for you?"

"Yes."

"Do you mind him having all those other affairs?"

"Believe me, I give Michael everything he wants in bed."

"I think not. Let me show you something."

At night as Evangeline slept I followed Michael. I'd gathered quite a few shots of him with other women. None of them had Evangeline's qualities, but many were beautiful. I took her through into the living room and put the shots up on screen.

She stared in anger at the array of evidence that Michael was playing with her.

"As you can see, Evangeline, the pictures all have dates on them."

"You've been stalking me," she said. "How far does your sick obsession extend?"

"What are you more concerned about now, the fact that I know more about you than you'd like, or the fact that Michael is not who you think he is?"

"And who are you, who exactly are you Rex?"

"Michael's infidelity doesn't exist because you are not Evangeline with him, you are only Evangeline with me."

"And you want me to be Coral."

"You already are."

"You've trapped me and now you want to destroy my affair. Rex, you're taking over my life and I don't like it."

"Two hours a week, that's all. Your life is yours."

"Is it when I'm under observation?"

"You can still see Michael."

"Do you want to watch me with him?"

"I don't think Michael would appeal to Coral."

"Why?"

"You'll find out."

"You know, these two hours a week dominate my days."

"Why do you think that is, Evangeline?"

"I keep wondering who she is. When I'm with Harry I think how would Coral behave?"

"That's because you're a true professional."

"This is insane."

"What do you think Coral would do about Michael?"

"I think she'd use him."

I had her passion and now I had her insights.

"I think so too," I said.

"I think she'd take what she wanted and finish with him, move onto the next man."

"Do you think she hates men?"

"She despises them for how easy they are to use."

"How does she use them?"

"With her body, she can get whoever she wants into bed."

"What does she want from them?"

"Attention. Money."

"Pleasure?"

"Her pleasure lies in being number one."

"You see, you know her."

"I think Coral doesn't believe she's worth that much. The fact that men do demeans them in her eyes."

"Would she allow a man to misuse her?"

"No. She wants to control the attention she gets."

"What are you going to do about Michael?"

"I'll try Coral's way."

"Evangeline, you know all about her."

"You're changing me, Rex, I don't like this."

"I'm giving you the right atmosphere."

"The right atmosphere for what?"

"Look at yourself."

I took her by the shoulder. I turned her round so she was facing the mirror. And she stood staring at her new reflection.

She was Evangeline, her face beautiful and inviting, with anger and confusion there. In her short skirt and halter top she looked stunning and she paused to admire herself before she caught the look.

It was in the eyes. It's always in the eyes when you see the change. She knew then who she was.

"Your expression has changed," I said.

"Is that how she looked?"

"It is."

"So she was always watching."

"She must have been."

"Wanting to be watched."

"She had to be watched."

"How many years, Rex?"

"I don't know."

"You've made me too conscious of myself. I may stop giving parties altogether and remain unseen."

"You're not a good liar when you lie to yourself, only when you're conning Harry."

"If you think when I tell you who Coral is I'm talking about myself, you're mistaken."

"I saw the look on your face when you left Michael, it is a look you ever show Harry."

She looked at her watch.

"I'm accumulating a wardrobe. Harry thinks I'm on shopping expeditions."

"Does he care?"

"No. That's why I wear them at parties. But I'm accumulating more than a wardrobe, I'm gathering another woman's skin. I sometimes catch myself as I entertain and I say some phrase or word I never use. You're eroding some part of me."

"You know who Coral is, Evangeline."

21.

I didn't see it as erosion. How much does identity belong to us? It is based on unreliable things. Memory can be taken away. The character can be altered. Perhaps it was the vacuum in my soul that made me hunger for Evangeline, and devour her confusion. I also wanted to strip her, not sexually, but her being. I wanted to remove everything she'd placed there as props to the tired drama she was playing with Harry.

I moved into the second stage of costumes, the more exotic clothes that Coral wore. I had to buy them from designer shops. I knew her measurements, and details of her being that Harry would have never known.

I brought the camera out into the open. She was ready for that.

The covert one didn't produce the desired effect. The images were static and allowed only glimpses of her face.

"Evangeline, I am going to film our meetings," I said, one afternoon over lunch.

"Haven't you got enough films of me? All those hours of spying on me."

"Those were observation films."

"Rex, you have me here every week."

"I will film you as you become Coral."

"This is like being part of some freaky experiment. Harry said the other day I was acting strange."

"Strange how?"

"He didn't say. I felt he was implying I didn't sound like me."

"Do you think you're becoming someone else?"

"Oh, this is taking it too far. I'm Evangeline."

"Of course you are. And Coral."

22.

She was in the chrysalis stage. Her skin was like silk. Her face showed expressions unknown to those around her. All except me. I knew the secret Evangeline, the lost one, the one yet unbecome, the one I bred there on camera, the one I let live as the past unfolded its wings like a silent bat.

She gained definition by the day. She was already beautiful when I found her, stumbled upon her in the quiet Avenue. As she became familiar with Coral she blossomed into something more, something exotic and dangerous.

Coral was like an unknown pregnancy in Evangeline, a watchful presence inhabiting her body. She was an undiscovered aspect of her being, and I allowed Evangeline to become her. Those sides of her she didn't like, those pieces she'd brushed aside, all the unwanted fragments of her being stored in the shadows cast by the breezeless trees of Broadlands Avenue began to lay claim to her.

The becoming. That is film. The moving images tell a story. They show the unfolding of a character. The unknown in her began to act its part, as I knew it would, when I inserted the key of watchfulness into the space between Evangeline and her past. It was like a fissure that spread in the edifice of a building and it was happening too fast. The flickering into life of Coral was like the rapid beat of light in a strobe effect. I had to slow her down. I had to make her Coral.

And so I filmed her. She was awkward at first, resentful of the self-consciousness the presence of the camera engendered in her. Slowly she relaxed into it, the role I knew she was destined to play the first time I set eyes on her.

"How do you want me to act?" she said the first day I began filming.

We were in the living room, the doors to the terrace were open and a light breeze drifted in from the arid garden where the grass lay yellowing in the sun. She was sitting in a light white skirt and blouse and uncrossed her legs.

"As you have been," I said.

"You want me to play the part of a woman, and you don't know who she is. I have no lines."

"You have all her lines, Evangeline, you just need to discover her in yourself."

"Is this some psychological game you're playing? Asking me to become someone else?"

"Why would I do that?"

"It's a way of undermining my identity."

"Do you think you're identity's being undermined?"

"I don't know what to think. I feel like a prostitute."

"Why?"

"Because you're booking my time and asking me to act out some fantasy."

"Coral is no fantasy."

The X unveiled her that day.

She tried out body language. She needed to use her body on me. She altered her mannerisms. But it wasn't her. None of it was Coral.

At times I felt on the precipice of the violent discovery I sought. At other times I felt intense frustration that Evangeline remained herself.

"How is Michael?" I said.

"I visited him, we made love, but it has changed."

"Do you feel betrayed by him?"

"I feel cold. I looked at him and saw he was a cheap mirror. I've decided to use him and then find another lover."

We went outside and she lit an Epique. In that moment she held the cigarette like her, her elbow in her left hand, the Epique poised in mid air. I knew it was Coral, sitting there in this other woman's body. Evangeline was now more alone than if she'd never found the company of men and felt so desired. For the presence of Coral parted Evangeline from herself that summer, and deprived her of her certainty in how she was desired. And as she altered, I became her focal point. She needed to hold onto something. We all do when the self is taken away.

I sometimes wondered what I was in those days. A doctor, perhaps, I thought. I considered my relationship with Evangeline. She needed things from me, much like a patient needs them from her doctor. I thought perhaps I was a criminal, or a businessman with a taste for certain women. I might have been a scientist, intent on studying the human race. But I was none of these.

That is how I found Coral, piece by missing piece, that long summer when Evangeline altered.

I held the camera as she sipped her wine, searching for her position.

"What would you do if Harry found out?" she said.

"About this?"

She nodded.

"I'm having lunch with a neighbour," I said.

"Where do you think this is going, Rex? Our meetings can't go on forever."

"What do you think Coral would do?"

"I think Coral does exactly what she wants."

"And what do you want?"

"I want another cigarette, Rex."

The tone of her voice then was Coral's. As she removed her lighter from her bag I grabbed her arm. I had to see it.

It was a chrome lighter, which bore the name of an unfamiliar brand.

"What are you doing?" she said, pulling her hand away.

I heard a gunshot. Behind the cloud of smoke her face looked like a mask.

"You're sweating, Rex," she said.

I looked at her fingers, and followed the arc of her arm as she smoked, drawing myself back into the present again. She stood up and stubbed out the cigarette beneath her heel.

"This is getting too creepy," she said.

All afternoon after she left I replayed the film on the X, in the living room with a glass of wine.

The images were crystal clear. Evangeline's face changed as she sat there in my house. She was playing the part and she was doing it so well I questioned who she really was. She had a range of expressions and I tried to pick out which were hers and which were Coral's.

PLAYING WITH GLASS

23.

The following evening they had another party. Harry invited me over. I saw him on the drive and he said, "Rex, haven't seen you in a while, join us tonight."

I went because I wanted to observe her in the company of others. I wanted to see how much she was still Evangeline. It's such a subtle thing, identity. And when the things we use to adorn it fall like leaves, the beauty of the exposure is equal to the sense of loss.

I arrived early and watched her as she smoked at the end of her garden. It was as if she always held a cigarette in her hand in those burning days. And it seemed what was being scorched was knowledge of ourselves, as if the sun was intent on getting beneath the skin. Harry was setting out a table. He handed me a glass of Sauvignon Blanc. I watched her as I drank it. I heard it in her voice as she greeted her guests. Evangeline's expressions no longer seemed her own.

Coral was entering her. Coral enters everyone after a while. It wasn't so much the words Evangeline used as the emphasis she placed on them, as if her interests lay elsewhere than the places that typified her character. The accents of speech say much about a person's views and habits. Evangeline's manner of delivery was changing.

She avoided me all evening. Every time I approached her she would begin a conversation with another guest.

Samantha was there, drunk. She cornered me. She talked endlessly of things I half listened to. She wanted my attention. She lifted up a pained face and told me about Kevin.

"He's been seeing this woman," she said. "I found out last week. He's with her tonight."

I wanted to get rid of her, she was blocking my view of Evangeline.

"What do you intend to do about it?" I said.

"I won't leave the bastard, why should I give up my lifestyle? But I intend to bed the first available man, Rex."

She was holding my arm as she said this and I was looking over her shoulder at Evangeline, who was saying something in a loud voice to Harry that I couldn't hear. I wanted to walk over and listen to their conversation. Harry marched off and Evangeline mingled with the guests. I could see she was on edge and I wondered what the dispute was about.

She more alive with me, on film, more Coral, more real, than here, alone among those who misunderstood her. I wanted to leave the party.

Samantha must have seen me watching her.

"They all want to look at her," she said, with a sneer. "I could tell you things about her. Evangeline is not all she pretends to be, I knew her before she met Harry."

She had my attention then. I looked at her, and knew she was on offer. She was wearing a low cut dress and she looked attractive, desperate, lonely and angry. She wanted revenge and I wanted knowledge.

She laid her hand on my arm.

"I like talking to you, Rex."

"It's a bit hard to hear you with all these bodies milling about. Let's go to my house for a drink."

She put her glass down and followed me along the side passage. Evangeline and Harry were nowhere to be seen as we left.

Samantha was swaying as she removed her shoes and sat down on my sofa. I watched her tuck her feet beneath her. I felt displaced by her presence. Her mannerisms seemed alien. I realised then that the only other person to have sat there was Evangeline and I looked at Samantha as if she was an impostor.

I handed her a glass of Meursault.

"Nice place," she said.

"What were you saying about Evangeline?"

"Why is everyone so interested in her?"

"Are they?"

"The men all are. Maybe she'd like the women to be more interested."

"She seemed a bit on edge tonight."

"She's been acting strangely recently."

"There seems to be some tension between her and Harry."

"Huh, little does he know."

Samantha stood up and began to wander around the house. I followed her, watching as she looked at the rooms.

"I like you, Rex," she said in the hallway, putting her hand on my chest. "What's upstairs?"

She went up and found the bedroom and lay on the bed. I'd closed the door to the spare room, where Evangeline dressed as Coral. There were clothes waiting for her in there and I went into the master bedroom after Samantha, wanting to stop her from exploring further. She was looking up at me as I touched her leg.

"S'nice," she said, her eyes dreamy.

Her mouth was open and I kissed her. She pulled at my shirt and I ran my hand up her thigh.

Her body was full of desperation and greed. I could feel her fear of aging as I touched her skin. She was an attractive woman, in her own way. But she was diminished by Evangeline's orbit, like all the others.

The experience made me think of acting. And it made me think of Evangeline becoming Coral.

Afterwards she lay there looking at me.

"At least I like men," she said. "Maybe that's why Kevin did it. I think he's always been nervous I'd stray."

"We've not been particularly discreet."

"I suppose this mustn't happen again."

"Unless you want to be found out."

"I don't."

"Do you think Evangeline would tell Kevin if she saw you leaving here?"

"Oh no. She wouldn't want me telling her little secret."

"That she has affairs?"

"Maybe. But no, there's something else, something I know about her. I knew her years ago. When she liked women."

"Evangeline is a lesbian?"

"I think she swings both way, Rex. Whether she still does, I don't know, but she used to enjoy women, and how."

She started to get dressed. And as she covered her large breasts with her bra I felt desire for her. I wanted to tear off her clothes and have her body again. But it was Evangeline's nakedness I sought in Samantha's revelations. She'd left me hungry for more information about Evangeline's past.

24.

Evangeline stayed away between visits. She told me pieces of her life, the bits that favoured her vanity. And if the part she played for me was in conflict with her being, then by telling me who she was, she was beginning the act of re-claiming herself from Coral. Evangeline carefully controlled what she revealed about herself. She would not enjoy the knowledge that I'd slept with a friend of hers who out of chagrin had let loose information aimed at reducing her appeal.

But her appeal was not lost. There was more to be shown and I knew it, I knew behind those eyes was another woman entirely and Coral had begun to drag her out bit by bit into the daylight of the studio that was The Telescope.

I continued to film her when she didn't know. I wanted to catch the pieces she still hid.

What I noticed on the secret films I took of her in those weeks was that Coral was inhabiting her more and more. She didn't recognise the level to which she'd been altered.

She was more relaxed when she knew the camera was on her, than when she was alone, unaware that the X was capturing her. It was as if she'd succumbed to the need to be filmed. A star needs to be naked on screen while holding back that final piece that makes viewers yearn for her.

The next week she met me one evening and we dined on an array of cold seafood.

"Sometimes I feel I tell you more about myself than I do Harry," she said.

"And why do you think that is?"

She laid her fork down and gave me a searching look.

"I don't know, Rex. This whole thing is so weird."

"I think you're learning who you are, who you really are, Evangeline."

"I know who I am."

"Then why are you changing?"

"You've got me acting Coral, and at times she seems to take me over. I can be with Harry and say something or do something that pulls him up. He's suspicious of me now, watchful. I feel alone because he doesn't know what you do, my secret that you found out and hold over me. Before you found it out it didn't matter, because it was mine alone. But now I feel it's shared, and your knowledge has made me too self-conscious of it all. And I feel you're the only person I can disclose things to. Now my husband probably suspects I'm conducting an affair."

"Are you?"

"Sometimes I wish I was with you. Sometimes I wish I just came over here and you fucked me and we talked. It would be easier. I'm used to that, to the disguises necessary to not being found out. But this is like some excision of me, some digging into who I really am. It makes me feel naked in ways I had never thought possible."

"Are you still seeing Michael?"

"Yes."

"Has he said you're different?"

"He hasn't, but he's thinking it."

"How well do you think you know Coral?"

"This is ridiculous, this woman may not exist. You may have come here, spied on me, now you've trapped me and you're playing some game with my being. I don't know who Coral is. I've known about myself for a long time."

"What have you known?"

"When I was a teenager I knew how beautiful I was. It isn't hard, men look at you, boys want your company, girls less attractive all want you to be their friend. I knew then what I had and I used it. I let men take me out, I had sex with them, often men much older than me, I ignored the teenage boys. They couldn't give me what I wanted."

"What did you want?"

"I wanted to feel expensive and exclusive."

"So what's different now, Evangeline?"

"I want my price tag to be known."

"By you or other people?"

"With Coral I don't feel in control."

"Do you think Coral's in control?"

"She doesn't exist does she, Rex?"

I looked away.

"She does," I said.

"I tell you something I know about Coral, if I saw her I'd hate her on sight."

25.

Samantha's revelation became a lens through which I viewed Evangeline. I wondered what she would do if her status was sufficiently threatened. Evangeline would use her body in whatever ways advantaged her. I considered that she despised sex for its cheapness. I contemplated the nature of her physical reality, her body's need and the manner in which she used it. And it seemed to me her skin was a mask beneath which lay the thing I'd hunted with the camera. Man's need for penetration goes deeper than flesh. I'd changed Evangeline, I'd modelled her on Coral. Or perhaps she'd already been that way and allowed me to watch her denude herself to her erotic core.

She played to the camera. She gazed at the X, her eyes filled with knowledge of her appeal. She talked to me of things she'd never tell Harry. And I listened to them argue at night. Voices were raised and windows slammed shut in the violent, intrusive heat. I'd see Harry leave the next day, tense and angry. Evangeline would follow some time later, her sunglasses hiding her eyes as she went shopping or, I imagined, to meet Michael, who may have redeemed the pieces Harry chipped away. Their marriage was feeling the exposure. Harry sensed the unseen drama from which he was excluded.

I had no interest in pursuing her. I held her in my palm. I saw her sinking in those weeks. She revived when she saw me. For The Telescope became the one place where she didn't need to hide. She was resentful in the trap I'd set, and grateful for the freedom it allowed her.

The next week she came to lunch wearing a white Fendi skirt and blouse. It was over100 degrees, and we sat on my terrace.

"Harry's away, I think he's taken a mistress," she said.

"What makes you say that?"

"He doesn't touch me anymore."

"Do you want him to?"

She didn't answer, and I wondered how many other lies she told me. I knew most of them. I knew too much, you see. I'd heard Harry enter Evangeline the night before. It was too hot to sleep and I was standing by the fountain when I heard his exaggerated sexual groans break across the dry grass like an inarticulate stutter. Evangeline didn't moan at all with him, and I thought of the gasps she made for Michael, captured on tape, as she was captured now.

In her marriage, Evangeline was still running the show. She had Harry just where she wanted him. But she didn't have me. I held the camera and it set her at a distance.

She began to talk to the X more and more. It sat on tables, perched on shelves, and she would turn to it as if it were a silent confidant.

In close up shots, she would try to talk to me beyond the lens. She wanted to seduce it, she wanted to feel it glide across her skin. She dwelt in the optical shadow of Coral. Evangeline needed to reach me, I always knew that.

That day of static heat we ate little.

"Let's go into the living room, Rex," she said.

I went to get some wine.

When I returned Evangeline was taking off her clothes.

"Is this how you want me, Rex?" she said, slipping out of her skirt. "You can have me, don't you want to touch me?"

She removed her blouse.

"I don't want you in that way," I said.

She unhooked her bra and peeled off her G-string.

Her body took my breath away. Although I'd seen her naked on film there was no camera between us.

"How much do you lie to yourself, Rex?" she said.

I poured some wine, but she'd seen my desire.

When I turned around she was standing next to me. She took my hand and put it on her skin.

26.

We didn't speak, it was just our bodies talking then. There was only darkness and desire.

I thought about how she would be on film, if her sexuality could be shown there. But the things Evangeline was to reveal to me belonged to privacy and the isolated hours when we showed our passions and the roles fell away like our clothes. The hunger I felt for her was overwhelming.

In the darkness with only the yielding contours of her body, I knew I wanted her. Deprived of watchfulness, my sense of touch told me of the craving I'd held in my heart. I saw my reflection in the mirror briefly afterwards, before I looked away. I didn't want to remember how I looked then. I was someone else, not Rex, the man behind the lens. Evangeline had brought me to life through the body, and some sentient part of me began to ache.

Afterwards she said, "So, Rex, what now? Now that you've had me."

"Have I had you, Evangeline, or is it the other way around?"

I caught a furtive and knowing glance in her face. It reminded me of an early look she gave me when she first invited me to her parties at the beginning of that endless summer. I looked at her full, inviting breasts, the arc of her hips as she lay on her side, and I craved more.

Evangeline was trying to take control. I had to start filming again. I needed to observe her.

The texture and smell of her skin acted as a stimulant to my memory and I went to wash. But as I turned the shower on, bile rose to my mouth and I stood there watching the steam fill the bathroom. The smell of Evangeline's cigarette drifting across the hallway was a comfort then.

After I dressed I found her on the terrace. She was looking out at the black yawning garden and said to me, "Do you want me to be her in bed, is that what you want, do you want Coral to fuck you?"

27.

I couldn't wash for several days. I felt punctured by a splinter of the past and I drank to remove it. I waited for Evangeline to return, vowing not to touch her, but to continue filming, to continue with the game of Coral.

Evangeline was penetrating my mind, and I felt Coral deep inside her. I wanted to find out more, and I thought about what Samantha had told me.

Desire comes in many forms. It is often embodied in the things we seek to control or acquire in pursuit of other objectives. While I took what Samantha could offer me, I desired her. The appeal of her nakedness was more than physical, it was a path to the heart of Evangeline. Samantha was, in herself, a form of foreplay.

One evening I forced myself to wash and called her. She came over and I tried to recreate the passion I felt for Evangeline as I touched her naked body. She needed reassurance that she was desired and I wanted information. We traded our bodies till dawn.

I asked for nothing, and her native spite towards Evangeline blossomed in the attention she received.

"I haven't seen you at the last parties," she said, as we lay there afterwards.

"I'm tired of them."

"Tired of Evangeline, who everyone wants?"

"Not me."

"I can't see the appeal. Yes, she's attractive, but..."

"She likes women."

"She did. When she was younger."

"How well do you know her?"

"I know she's got a temper. When pushed."

"I've heard her and Harry arguing, she always sounds contained."

"I think it would take a woman to bring out Evangeline's aggression."

"Did something happen between you?"

"No. I've always stayed on the right side of her. And I like her in a way, I like the parties, and I feel slightly sorry for Harry, having to watch her all the time. But if Evangeline feels upstaged she'll fight."

"You mean physically?"

She nodded and I waited for her to continue, wondering if I'd made it too clear where my interests lay.

"She had mental problems as a young woman. I'm not sure what they were, but she used to change a lot, moody. She seemed to be a series of people at the parties we both went to, as if she was trying out different roles. She took drugs, the usual recreational stuff. I think they affected her. She seemed better when she stopped taking them. There were a lot of scenes when I saw her in bed with men and women. She was the one they all wanted. We were part of a crowd. There was one incident I remember, when this rather stunning, younger woman turned up. She took some of the spotlight. Evangeline hated that. One night they argued. She told Evangeline she wasn't that special. Evangeline hit her. Hard. It wasn't just a slap. She lashed out fiercely. If you ever see Evangeline upstaged you'll know what I mean. Or maybe she's changed."

"Why would she need to change?" I said.

She didn't answer.

She lay next to me in the twilight, and her body looked hollow. The knowledge she'd imparted had emptied her of appeal.

After she left I lay in bed thinking of Evangeline. I wanted her, and Coral.

* * *

Time didn't move between Evangeline's visits. I existed in a vacuum of static observation. I moved around my empty home, watchful and fearful of the sound of water. I hated listening to the parties when her guests would splash around in the swimming pool and I longed for the weather to break so that the festivities would end. I wondered what she would look like in autumn, under a grey sky. And perhaps it was the heat and the nature of the light that brought about the series of events that lost summer.

Evangeline stopped wearing the outfits I picked for her. She began to wear her own. She'd amassed a huge wardrobe with what Harry thought resentfully was his own money. Now she chose what she considered Coral would wear. And I let her. I let her become her.

Evangeline turned up the following week for lunch dressed in a floral skirt and blouse. It was subtle and erotic, it was Coral. It was evident she was not wearing a bra and she looked at me with decision in her eyes, as if she'd resolved where this was going.

"Do you still need to film me, Rex?" she said.

"I need you on film until you're her."

"Has it occurred to you that she may only reveal herself in bed?"

"This is just your way of taking over."

"I'm not your object, Rex. Is that what Coral was?"

"I don't know who she is."

"Is?"

"Sometimes she's standing right in front of me."

"What do you want from Coral?"

"The past."

I'd said it before I realised the sense of the word and it lay swollen on my tongue.

I existed in fragments in those days. I caught snatches of myself like disconnected parts of a song.

I took the X and set it before her as we ate. All through lunch the sound of a dripping tap made sweat run down my back.

Her performance that day was exquisite. She was Coral as she stood up and said, "Rex, can you light my cigarette?"

She was standing on the threshold of the terrace door and she passed beyond it as I took her lighter from the table. It almost burned my hand as I glanced at the word "Diva" on its polished surface and stepped outside into the heat.

I set the flame to her Epique and saw the fire in her eyes as she blew smoke into my garden. She was a star, and she knew it. There was something eternal in her gestures.

In that moment the fountain of Hermes became menacing. I thought I saw a shadow in the gushing water and I went inside the house to the cool of the living room.

She came through and stood in front of me.

"Come to Coral," she said.

I watched as she unbuttoned her blouse. I rose. My hands were on her breasts and my tongue deep in her mouth, searching for an answer.

She took me by the hand and led me upstairs, and I felt the house was more hers than mine and I was merely a stranger there hunting for clues.

She stood in my sterile bedroom and removed her skirt and came over to me and unzipped my flies. She had me in her hand as she said, "Coral will fuck you now, Rex."

When I entered her that afternoon she became someone else.

There was a hardness in her eyes.

"What did she do for you, Rex?" Evangeline whispered in my ear as she climbed on top of me, her legs tight around me as she pushed my chest down onto the bed.

"It's more what she took away."

"Why the watchfulness, Rex? You can see all of me now, I'm your mistress today. Harry will fuck this body tomorrow, maybe tonight, Michael this week, but you have me here and I can be Coral for you if you tell me who she is."

"She is the endless watchfulness of my dreams."

I never filmed the sex. It was not part of the film.

I needed that one image of Coral staring out of Evangeline's eyes. And I was going to get it.

28.

I continued to film her secretly. As she wandered about her garden, inhaling her cigarette she even looked like another woman, distant, still, waiting for some event that loomed on the horizon.

We existed in those days in sweltering conditions that made people keep their windows open, allowing neighbours to overhear conversations previously kept private. Identities and secrets became revealed. Most of them were unimportant, small things kept safe from watchful eyes. Her arguments with Harry worsened. One night I heard him shout the word "affair" at her. Silence ensued, then raised voices. I knew Evangeline's behaviour had changed and Harry was observing it day by day, drawing the obvious, erroneous conclusion.

One morning he left early for work. I heard his wheels spin stones on the gravel drive and I looked out of my bedroom window to see Evangeline sitting with her legs in the pool. She was wearing a pink blouse and she turned to look at her garden. I zoomed in on her eyes and for a second they looked a different shade of green, not hers, but someone else's. Coral was penetrating Evangeline, who was ultimately more feminine.

She came to see me later that day. Beneath the surface of her eyes another woman watched me.

"Harry has accused me of having an affair," she said.

"Do you think he knows about Michael?"

"No, or he would have mentioned him."

"Then what are you worried about?"

"What he will do."

"Stop seeing Michael."

"That's what you've wanted all along."

"No."

"Rex, you've fucked me, you've taken my time and altered me in some way I can't define. I feel like I'm losing shape, what more do you want?"

"I want you to see yourself on film."

"I have."

"The film's not ready yet."

She went to pour herself some wine. It was barely midday.

"I'm drinking more and more."

"What is disturbing you?" I said.

"I feel invaded."

"What do you want?"

"My body. I want my body to feel like my own again."

"The thing you've always managed to use to your advantage. What changed?"

"Coral's changed me and I don't know who she is."

"Evangeline, you need to make love to Coral to find that out."

I knew that if I brought desire into her distaste for Coral I would have the film.

"How would Coral touch you, Rex?"

"I don't know."

"Like this?"

She began to drag the tips of her fingers down my temple.

"No," I said, "that was not the way."

"How then?"

"How often do you feel her when you are alone?"

"Too often."

"Then you should know how Coral touches and likes to be touched."

"But I don't, Rex, I don't."

29.

I gathered she stopped seeing Michael around this time. Her trips away from her house became less frequent. I heard her alone during the day listening to music. I smelt her smoke drift into my garden as I sat sipping chilled Meursault, waiting for the heat to stop.

But it didn't, not until it was all over and Coral came alive in only the way she knew how. She always brought drama with her, as if she couldn't exist without it.

Evangeline visited me the following week one evening for dinner. I knew as she arrived that despair was mounting in her.

"You know, Rex, the only time I feel free and unwatched now is in this prison you've made for me."

"That's because I've allowed you to be yourself."

"You've turned me into Coral."

"You exist on film."

"When I first came here, I felt so on edge and angry with you. I hated the idea you'd trapped me, caught me out, and I wondered how I could get out of this as fast as possible. Then you started filming me and I thought you were the sickest man I'd ever encountered. Harry wants to own everything. But now I feel his watchfulness is worse than this. He scrutinises me about the house, I don't know what he's thinking. He may have something planned. I come here and you film me, I can say what I want."

"Because I know everything about you."

"But I didn't give that knowledge to you willingly."

"You needed someone to have it."

"Rex, Harry is a dangerous man. I've seen him get people hurt."

"Are you worried for Michael?"

"I don't want to lose my marriage."

"Do you really think Harry would leave you?"

"I don't want to become Coral, Rex. I know he'll stay with me. And I'm concerned that if I lose myself I'll lose him."

"You're playing a part."

"Would Coral leave Harry?"

"I think she would."

"What else would she do, Rex?"

"Much more than we realise, Evangeline."

"So here we are, trying to define this woman who may not exist, who you may have made up to play games with my life, while my marriage crumbles and you film me."

"She does exist."

"Does she? Who is she?"

"I've seen her inside you."

"And so has Harry."

She was trying to light a cigarette and her lighter failed. I'd noticed it was temperamental and was ready for the scene.

"Have you got a match, Rex?"

I fetched it from the living room.

"I thought you might like this," I said.

"Zippo. You think I'm a Diva?"

"I like the crystal in the middle."

She ignited its first violent flame as she kept her eyes locked on mine, and her cigarette crackled in the burning air.

"I do like it, it seems so fitting to what we're doing."

"And what do you think that is, Evangeline?"

"Making me into someone else, of course."

Evangeline tried to reclaim herself as the sunshine denied any reprieve in the heat. But she was not Coral, not yet.

30.

The following midnight I heard the sound of breaking crockery. I'd just lain down when the noise broke through the sleeping stillness of the garden. The initial thought of an intruder and how to deal with him was displaced by Evangeline's voice. She sounded afraid.

"Harry, stop!"

"You're not doing this to me," he yelled.

Then suddenly silence fell on their row like a blanket being dropped on a fire. I got out of bed.

I stared out of my window at their house. All the lights were on and a white blur flew across the garden. It was Evangeline in her nightie. Harry was chasing her in his underpants along the edge of the pool. She dodged him until he grabbed her next to the steps beneath which the clear blue water shone. The underwater lights sparkled like submerged stars.

Harry was holding Evangeline by her arms, if he let go she would have fallen in. I felt my cosmos reverse, as if I existed in the mirror image of some faded reality. I watched with a dry mouth as Harry dragged her across the patio and into the house.

Then I heard the French doors slamming shut.

I considered how much I was a part of what was happening.

I had to stop Harry maiming her. I put on some clothes and raced out onto my drive.

A police car was drawing up outside the Glass's house. Two officers got out.

"I heard a disturbance," I said.

"Please wait there, Sir," one officer said.

I watched them enter the house. I waited, inhaling midnight like a sin. I was about to go back into The Telescope when I saw them leave. Harry was standing at the doorway in a bath robe that hung open.

He saw me and came out. His eyes were hollow.

"It's Evangeline," he said. "She's having an affair."

"I'm sorry, Harry," I said.

31.

I had to hold onto the image. We all need a constant in our world. All night Evangeline's face burned in my mind. Her skin bubbled and broke open, and by dawn she was a skeleton in rags, clutching at my legs as I ran from her. I woke with bile in my mouth and turned on the shower, afraid to wash.

I had some Blue Label I'd been saving and poured two fingers into a tumbler, swallowing its fire as I stepped into the steaming water. I scrubbed myself, shivering with fear beneath the heat. Then I dressed.

I watched her on film. I replaced the images of her damaged face with the ones I kept in my house like syringes filled with morphine.

The idea that Harry would harm her made me sit all morning staring at the screen, drinking whisky. When I heard the door chime I didn't expect her, but I smelt her perfume as I stood in the hallway. She was wearing her sunglasses and as she stepped into The Telescope I imagined her eyes blackened by Harry's fists. She stood there briefly, saying nothing as I looked at her. And the strangest thought entered my head. *If Evangeline had planned her seduction of me as Coral, she would have waited until now to strike.*

Seductions don't take place in the bedroom, they occur in our minds before the physical act. And in that moment I knew how much better Evangeline was than the thing I sought. I stood there looking into her shades, wanting her physically in a way I never had until that day.

She removed them slowly. It was like the first time she stripped in front of me.

There was not a mark on her skin. She looked more beautiful than ever, and there was a glint of triumph in her eyes.

"Drink, Rex? Or am I too late?" she said.

I went through into the kitchen and opened a bottle of Meursault. She sipped it slowly in the living room. It was our room and I felt as though Coral didn't belong there.

I sat down opposite her.

"I saw Harry last night," I said.

She pointed to her frozen image on the screen.

"You've been watching me again."

"I could tell he doesn't suspect anything between us."

"No, he doesn't think it's happening under his nose. But he is convinced I am having an affair."

"Did he hurt you?"

"No. He frightened me, but I dealt with it."

"What did you do?"

"I didn't do anything. Coral did it all. And I have to thank you for that because if she hadn't been there last night, I may have got hurt."

"What did Coral do?"

"She called the police, something I would never do."

"Why not?"

"Bad experience years ago when I did drugs. I got busted, one of the police officers felt me up in the cell. I've never considered involving the police in my affairs. Besides, I believe I can handle Harry."

"And you felt Coral directed you to make the call?"

"She told me to."

I looked at her there in my living room and she was wearing someone else's face. She was Coral, as summer swelled as if its invisible skin was cracking.

"What do you think has made him suspicious?"

"Coral taking me over."

"He has no evidence that you are seeing Michael?"

"No."

"Then you just need to reassure Harry that you are not being unfaithful."

"It's not that, Rex, he found something."

"What?"

"He was looking for my lighter and found a clear blue in my bag."

"A pregnancy kit?"

"With the word pregnant on it. I told him it was Samantha's, and that she'd asked me to get rid of it for her, but he didn't believe me."

"Are you pregnant?"

"Yes."

"Whose is it?"

"The kit even said 2-3weeks. It's yours, Rex."

"How do you know it's not Harry's or Michael's, Coral?"

"Evangeline Rex, it's Evangeline. Harry's sterile."

"You told me you couldn't have kids."

"No, I said we couldn't have kids, I was covering for Harry."

"Why not Michael's?"

"Because I was too angry to have sex with him for a long time after your revelation of his betrayal. The last time I slept with him was a few days ago, after I got pregnant with your child."

"Whose does Harry think it is?"

"He doesn't know. But it's yours, Rex, two weeks ago you were fucking me upstairs, remember?"

"So what are you going to do, Evangeline?"

She looked at me with momentary incomprehension. Her eyes looked as hard as gemstones.

"Abort it, of course."

32.

I paid.

I'd been paying for years. I wrote the cheque feeling sick and looked at Coral standing there in a blue chiffon dress, peering out at me beneath Evangeline's skin. There was no place for motherhood here. The air was full of broken seeds and my stomach did a revolution, as I felt lost beneath a turning wave.

"This way I can make Harry doubt it all," Evangeline said. "If I'm not pregnant and he has no evidence of an affair then we're home free."

"Are we?"

"Rex, I don't want children."

"Then what?"

"Finish the film."

I watched her walk away with a piece of my soul in her belly. She returned later smelling of chemicals. Even at my closed window from which I watched her slither up her drive, she stank.

I had to drive the smell away with whisky.

I didn't watch any films of her that day, but sat alone looking at the pictures of my daughter.

Harry was clipping one of the Beech hedges on their drive. The staccato metal noise made me think of bullets being loaded into the chamber of a rifle. I was sweating by the time he stopped. I enjoyed the silence of the evening.

Then a party start started next door. As music drifted out across Broadlands Avenue, and the idle guests wandered into the Glass's garden, my brain played me Fleetwood Mac's "The Chain."

I broke two windows to drive the sound away. I threw a chair and ripped the plasma screen off the wall, hurling it into the garden, where the shards of glass fell like broken stars.

33.

I bought another plasma screen. I got the window fixed. I thought about the nature of glass. I heard dripping taps in The Telescope and coursed along the empty corridors with the echo of the song in my brain, making sure no water was leaking into the sinks. I rubbed them with towels and ran my palms across the tiles to ensure they were dry. But my mind showed me things, vast empty spaces filled with water and falling bodies. They made me think of the void Evangeline had created inside herself, and I began to drink each morning to shut them out.

My drunkenness didn't go unnoticed by Evangeline. Her sex life outside the studio of my house, until then a subject of irrelevance to me, now began to trouble me and leave me tasting salt tears in the swollen midnights when I lay alone seeing images that left me sweating in the dark. I'd spy on her continually and nearly followed her one day, suspecting she was visiting Michael.

We passed a silent lunch together when she said little and left as soon as the two hours were up.

"I'm going to make one last visit," she said that day, "and then this is going to stop."

"It stops when the film is finished."

But she was already Coral. Her face was hard and beneath her eyes lay calculation and deceit.

I watched the transformation on film, the gradual entrance by Coral into Evangeline until she inhabited her body.

Evangeline had more than one lover. Michael enjoyed her while I feasted on her flesh and Harry fell apart. Coral too enjoyed her body for a while.

* * *

I hadn't heard from Samantha since that second time. When Evangeline mentioned her name I momentarily wondered if she knew I'd slept with her, and if Samantha might be pregnant. Her silence was reassuring. I imagined I'd restored some of her injured self-worth and she'd recovered from the compromise.

The next day I received an invitation to dinner.

I was getting out of my car when Alberta called to me from the street.

"I've been ringing their bell," she said. "Have they gone away?"

I looked over at the Glass's house.

"We're having dinner tonight, do come, Rex."

I surprised myself in accepting.

Later that evening, I drove the few minutes' distance to the Smythes' address, wondering what Evangeline was doing. Alberta answered the door in a burgundy dress that made her look too thin. Her skin tone was wrong for the colour, and the cut was shapeless. I looked over her shoulder at Brad, who was striding up the hallway to greet me.

"Rex, glad you could make it," he said, extending a hand, as I stepped into their house.

I handed him the bottle of Meursault I'd brought with me.

"Very nice," he said, ushering me into the living room.

There were six of us that tired evening, when I felt more displaced than ever. The people I knew at Evangeline's parties were dulled by her absence.

A small man called Tom who sported a beige shirt and snorted regularly between sentences bored me in the tasteless living room that lacked all character or thought. Brad was wearing some tight fitting chinos that showed his angular ankles beneath yellow socks that sat like egg yolks on his patent leather shoes.

For a time all I could hear was their creaking as he meandered about the room, pouring drinks and handing out broken crisps and stale nuts.

Alberta's attempts at sophistication brought on waves of nausea in me.

"Such a shame the Glasses can't be here," she said, waving her hand in the air, as if she was swatting a fly.

Tom snorted as if she'd told a crude joke. I wondered where they were. Perhaps they'd gone away and Alberta knew, arranging the dinner in a sick attempt to take the spotlight in Evangeline's absence.

I was thinking how Brad and Alberta looked like clockwork toys, when the bell went and Samantha and Kevin arrived. Her awkwardness was matched only by Kevin's ignorance.

After the usual pleasantries were exchanged, Kevin held forth about his recent business transactions. Samantha avoided my eyes, sitting forward on a chair in a black dress that made her look like a waitress. Tom sat next to her.

"Business is booming," Kevin said, "I'm making money hand over fist."

He elaborated about various deals that had fallen into his lap.

I saw beneath the ostentation the shadow of despair and wondered if a revelation had been made by Samantha.

"Harry's done well, hasn't he?" Alberta said.

Brad wagged a finger at her.

"He nearly got into trouble, though. Remember the time he used a bit too much muscle?"

Kevin looked at Brad.

"What time was that?"

"Before Evangeline, he'd made a lot, but there was one deal he was after and he didn't have the money. His rival ended up in a bad state."

"What do you mean?" Kevin said.

Brad clenched his fist.

"He had him done over. Harry's got a bit of a past."

"Haven't we all?" Tom said, and snorted, his small eyes on Samantha's cleavage, as she bent to fiddle with a strap on her shoe.

We ate some tasteless lamb and endured cheap wine.

I thought about the phrase Brad used.

"Before Evangeline" seemed to describe another continent, and I struggled with the sense of time. I wondered who I was before Evangeline and felt a sense of affinity for Harry.

I spoke to Samantha, briefly, only once that evening.

She was coming out of the toilet and I was in the hall.

"How are you Samantha?" I said.

"I made things up with Kevin."

"So it's all OK then."

"He stopped his affair, like I said he would."

"He never found out about you and me?"

"No. Affairs don't really suit me."

"I see."

"I'm not Evangeline, Rex."

She wasn't. No one was.

I watched her walk away, a middle aged woman with sadness in her gait, back to her brash husband.

I sat for a while longer while the conversation continued, and then left the small, poisoned suburban home and returned to the emptiness of The Telescope.

As I shut the door and went into the living room I could see glass from the broken window. Then I heard the opening notes of "The Chain."

34.

The constant crescendo of notes followed me around the empty house. Its insistence was maddening. It pursued me into dreams I wanted to leave behind, but which became more real than the days I spent waiting for Evangeline to turn up.

The following week I heard them argue again. Harry was yelling and I watched him storm off down the drive. His eyes were wet as he got into his car. His bravado had been stripped from him by something he had no knowledge of.

Evangeline came over that evening dressed in a tight black dress and coral pink blouse. All through dinner I watched her, my captive star, as she ate with precise and deliberate movements. She'd become her. I'd made steak and as she placed a rare morsel on her tongue I remembered Coral liked steak. For a moment I knew who she was, before some wave of forgetting submerged the knowledge.

We were standing in my living room after dinner, and I looked at Evangeline. Her face was hard and her beauty bore the look of lacquer, as if she'd varnished it to preserve a certain image. For a brief moment she seemed to have lost her range. The success of her performance brought with it the first taste of disappointment. Her confidence in the part she played seemed as fragile as glass.

"I know the lines, Rex."

"Why did you do it?"

"I didn't, you know that."

"Are you saying Coral aborted our child?"

"I'm saying it seems a fitting act for her." She walked up to me until she was inches from my face. "You know, Rex, if you alter someone in the way you've altered me, certain things will happen."

"Who are you, Evangeline?"

"I'm Coral. I live inside you."

"What do you want?"

"Everything, Rex."

In that moment she was her. In understanding Coral, Evangeline had gained her status again. It would be displaced suddenly, violently, by an event that would change her dramatically. Reality was about to penetrate the core of the dream.

"Why did you get rid of the baby?" I said.

"It was in my way."

"She could have been a star."

"She? Don't get sentimental on me, Rex."

"I heard you celebrating afterwards. You emptied your womb and partied."

"Why not? I fucked Harry that night. He's still suspicious. But the evidence is gone."

"So what am I, Evangeline?"

"The guy next door who films me."

She was walking towards the door when I came up behind her in the hall. That wasn't the ending I'd planned. She turned, and as I looked at her face I saw what I'd been trying to film all those burning weeks. And I knew that some things do not belong on film.

35.

She didn't come the following week. I considered going next door but I saw Harry's car there. It seemed he'd taken time off work. I imagined he'd brought his microscope and stretched Evangeline out on a slide, to study the nature of her lies.

I watched the films, all of them, from beginning to end. I stared for hours at the early covert ones I took of her alone, then the films of her visits. And I saw that as she began to play the part of Coral, what first had been a performance became second nature to her, as if she already knew her lines. I knew how pregnant with loss I'd been that summer, and I considered how little I knew.

Perhaps Coral and Evangeline were the same woman and I was being experimented on. My fragmented memory, my fear of water, made me feel like the actor in the drama. And all of it, from the first party, to sleeping with Samantha and Evangeline, seemed staged. At midnight I stepped out onto the cracked pavements of Broadlands Avenue and listened. The houses and lives were merely facades. Behind them I could hear the hidden machinery of theatre.

I saw a flash of water and smoke. The things that came to me were like the single notes of a song, but disconnected, paused, as if on a reel of tape that was stuttering into rhythm.

A narrative was breaking through the sequence of images. It was like finding someone's face in the dark. Coral was a fiction I was trying to make real when we began filming. But Evangeline knew her part. She knew it all too well in those unrehearsed meetings when she told me things about herself. A peculiar form of intimacy had developed between us, a prelude of what was to come. I had become her mirror. And her revelations were part of her need to manufacture an image. But that night it seemed to me I was the only spectator in the audience. Her party guests were actors in a drama whose meaning eluded me. Perhaps Harry was part of it. I tried to recall my old life before I arrived at the manufactured lie of Broadlands Avenue, and as I did, I felt guilt prick the surface of my skin.

I recalled the first time we had sex. I saw how she changed on film after that, as piece by piece she became Coral.

I spent an entire week watching the films as Evangeline stayed away. The arguments had stopped, there was little activity from next door. Then one day I saw her leave the house, and a car start up and follow her as she drove off.

And I still didn't know who Coral was in my life. I was about to find out.

ORIGINALS AND REPLICAS

36.

The weather broke for a day. Storm clouds rolled in, and the air filled with electricity. It seemed to be trying to animate something that was dead. I lay in bed seeing my room light up, counting the seconds between the thunder and lightning, feeling it approach. And I knew Evangeline would no longer play the part that had become so vital to my existence. I thought of the foetus as she stuffed pills into her vagina, the unwanted pulse between us removed on a wash of blood. I wondered how many pills she took, and I went downstairs and set 12 bottles of Meursault on the quartz worktop. As I looked at them I saw embryos floating behind glass in a museum.

What she'd taken from her womb had changed things and I felt the hollow sense of loss again as I wandered my house. It was lit up by a strobe effect as the lightning flashed, the objects and furniture looking uncertain, fragmented. I stared at my face in the bathroom mirror. I looked no more than an observer. I felt erased, and violated.

I slept and dreamed I was filming Coral. She moved beneath a flashing light. I kept asking her to play Evangeline, and her features looked flat and disappointing, as if she was a replica of the woman I had sought. We were on a busy set, with camera crews moving around her as she mouthed incomprehensible words. I became enraged and grabbed her face, removing a mask.

I awoke staring at blackness. The storm had stopped and outside the rain fell, but only until morning. I got up and looked out of the window. Harry's car was gone and there was no sign of Evangeline. By noon the sun had come out and the heat had risen. The puddles were drying. I thought of the lights of a film studio, and the make-up on the faces of actresses melting beneath them.

I went into the spare room and stared at the boxes I still hadn't unpacked. I began to open them, seeing reminders of the life I'd left when summer started, the bruised muscle of my memory throbbing.

37.

I saw Harry on his drive the next morning as I was getting into my car.

He walked towards me and stood on the other side of the low wall that separated our properties.

"I'm sure you've been disturbed by recent events," he said.

"People argue, Harry, I know that."

"The arguments will stop now, Rex," he said.

For a moment he became mysterious in his conviction. He'd always been a small and ugly fact next to Evangeline.

"You said something about an affair, Harry."

He shook his head.

"No more. You can continue to enjoy your time at The Telescope in peace," he said.

He couldn't have lied more if he'd tried. I watched him drive away, an ignorant man on the margin of a drama.

* * *

I was sipping the last of the Blue Label in the living room that evening when I heard the bell. I opened the door without hesitation, thinking it was Evangeline, and stood staring at a beautiful woman in a green blouse and white skirt, dark hair and emerald eyes.

There was something both exotic and unreal about her, as if she was a manufactured brand. She was filled with deliberation. And she looked famous. Shalini rose from her skin and drifted across the air.

I knew her, all right.

"Can I come in?" Coral said.

Outside on Broadlands Avenue a taxi pulled away.

She walked past me with a suitcase, and The Telescope suddenly seemed unreal. Coral went straight into the living room.

"Aren't you going to offer me a drink Rex?"

I poured her a glass of Sancerre and watched her sit down.

"How did you find me?" I said.

"It's not hard."

It was her. I'd searched for weeks for this woman who now sat in my house. And she was unwelcome. This thing I'd sought I wanted gone.

"What do you want?" I said.

"You think you can leave it all behind you, Rex?"

"I don't know who you are."

"You know my name."

"Yes, Coral."

"How much do you remember of what happened?"

She took out a Marlboro and lit it with the only lighter she could possess. She narrowed her green eyes at me as she snapped her Diva Zippo shut, took a long slow drag, and blew a plume of smoke at the ceiling.

I felt as though I was being questioned by someone with a record about me I wasn't privy to. A headache began to throb at my temple, and I left her to take a painkiller. I stood shaking in the bathroom, my hand clutching the sink's edge.

When I returned she was standing by the door to the terrace. With her back to me she could have been Evangeline, but as she turned I saw how different the two women were. Both were beautiful, both brunette with sexual self confidence written into their bodies, but Coral was hard in a way that Evangeline wasn't.

She walked towards me and held up her glass and I dutifully went and refilled it. I felt compelled to please her.

The temperature had climbed again and hot air entered from outside. I was sweating and Coral was as cool as marble.

As I looked at her it occurred to me that this was Evangeline, become Coral.

I remembered watching her back fade on a drive, an endless drive. The images I saw flickered like snapshots on the riffled pages of an album.

"It's only been a few weeks, Rex."

"Has it?"

"You have a nice house."

"And where have you been Coral?"

"Do you really not remember, or is this some elaborate game?"

"I remember you."

"Do you know who I am?"

"No."

She went over to the two pictures and picked one up. I wanted to snatch it from her hands.

"She was our daughter, Rex, you do remember that?" she said.

38.

"What happened to her?" I said.

"You really have forgotten."

"She died, I remember that."

Coral walked across the room and laid her hand on my shoulder. It seemed an unnatural gesture.

"Rex, let's have another glass of wine."

And so we sat in the living room filled with films of the wrong woman playing Coral, who was there now with me.

"What happened to Eve?" I said.

"You know your daughter's name, at least. Something happened, Rex. What do you remember?"

"Sometimes I hear gunshots."

"That's right."

She put her hand on mine. I found her tenderness unnerving.

"If I called you Donald Strike would it help you to remember?"

I knew the name. I felt like a child again, learning the words for things I saw around me, connecting the label to the object.

"Who is Donald Strike?"

"You, Rex. Or at least the name you worked under. You were a film director, a good one."

"Is the name I know assumed?"

"Your full name is Rex Donald Strike Allen."

"Eve was shot."

Coral nodded and I felt I was walking through a corridor blindfolded.

"She was."

"Why?"

"It was another party, Rex, another one of those evenings when our house was invaded by too many people."

"The house in Richmond?"

"Yes."

Memories were coming to me like troubled strangers.

"Who is Francis Merit?" I said.

Coral paused.

"I left you for him. I couldn't take anymore of your parties, the drugs. It didn't work, Rex. I'm back."

Coral began her account of events that lay beyond my memory and control.

"Tell me about the parties," I said.

39.

Coral sat before me, the living breathing player I'd searched for, a replica of Evangeline. I felt like an echo of myself. It was Evangeline I wanted as I listened to Coral talk of the past. Its shape was assuming clarity for me. I listened with a throbbing temple while she removed the fog I'd inhabited since I arrived at The Telescope. Coral changed summer with the past, the thing I'd lost before I came to Broadlands Avenue.

As Coral talked of the past and the events that led me there, I felt as though my reality was buckling.

"You had endless parties, Rex," she said. "You enjoyed the company. Actresses from your films thronged the poolside bar. You had producers, stars, actors looking to pull, and dealers." She laid a hand on my leg. "I know what fixes you, remember?"

"I don't."

"Some of them became orgies. Rex, you like watching."

As she spoke I felt as though she was raping my mind.

"Am I well known?"

"The name Donald Strike would be familiar to most movie goers. You're not a Hollywood director, but a rising star in the film world."

"How do I know any of this is true?"

"Google yourself."

I did and saw the Wikipedia entry and the list of my films on my website. I felt like a visitor in my own life.

"How come no one recognised me when I got here?"

"You were very private, you never gave interviews, there are hardly any pictures of you out there and those that are show you with a beard and sunglasses. Only people who worked with you would know what you look like."

"You mentioned drug dealers."

"Rex, you had a big habit, snorted coke all day. You existed in this freezing climate as if the air conditioning was on inside you. You stopped the coke, it made you paranoid. Then you put hidden cameras everywhere. You filmed everything, all part of what you called the endless movie of life."

"I remember that phrase."

"You even filmed me."

"We were married?"

"No."

"Why can't I remember?"

"You suffered a severe trauma, Rex."

40.

I watched her sleeping the second night she was there. She didn't belong on the spare bed, in the room where Evangeline dressed up as her. Her face looked tranquil and beautiful and I searched her skin for lies. I reached out and touched her leg and thought of touching Evangeline. The texture of their bodies was identical, but their eyes, although both green, were as distinct in expression as they could be.

There was no sexual connotation to any of Coral's movements as she went about the house getting dressed the next morning. She showed no embarrassment in displaying her partial nudity to me. I watched her putting on make-up and she caught my eye in the mirror as she continued with the steady application of lipstick, as if we were married and nothing had occurred between us.

I forgot about the house next door, and the world of Evangeline. It was as if I was back in Richmond, and the removal men hadn't arrived.

"A lot of the people who came to your parties were undesirable types," she said, as we ate breakfast. "Drugs were floating about the house and Eve got a habit young."

"How old was she when she died?"

"Sixteen."

A searing pain shot through my chest.

"What drugs was she using?"

"She found a stash of your coke and got hooked on it."

"My God."

I felt as though I was going to choke. I had to get away from Coral and I walked outside. The fountain smelled of chlorine and the landscape looked barren. I went back inside and stared at Eve's pictures.

Coral came up behind me. She touched me on the back and said, "Rex, you mustn't blame yourself."

"I'm a voyeur, a drug user whose daughter got hooked through his irresponsibility and I can't remember my own name. What does that make me, Coral? What else have I run from?"

And I looked at her, this woman I'd sought through that endless summer when the trees cast shadows across Broadlands Avenue and Evangeline entertained. There was nothing entertaining about Coral, but she enticed me with knowledge.

She was perfect, with all of perfection's harsh allure. She was the original and I'd been studying a replica. I looked at her hard green eyes and full lips. She was about to say something, she was about to tell me how Eve died and I took her face in my hands and placed my mouth on hers.

I knew in that moment that sexual desire is bound up in our knowledge of ourselves. And we are threatened in that knowledge. As we feel we fade we hunger for the physical. Men try to seal their identities with each moment of penetration, while women borrow time to maintain allure.

I peeled Coral's clothes off and found the body I knew so well. Upstairs I entered her on the same bed where I'd made love to Evangeline, with desperate desire. I heard her low slow gasps and watched her arch her back and everything was real for an hour as we swapped sins.

Her body was lean and tight beneath me, her touch passionate and calculated. Her sexuality was blatant and knowing. And as I filled her with the hot rush of my need I looked at her face and saw the most perfectly articulated whore I could have found, there, alone with me in my empty house, the bearer of truths that would end the film.

41.

She lay with me for a while before getting up. As I watched her dress she seemed to be acting.

Downstairs we drank coffee. The measured kindness with which she spoke may have been assumed, but I was grateful for it.

Coral sat on the sofa. I watched each gesture of hers, the simple way she raised her cup to her lips, and her familiarity became overbearing. The past was about to break through my fortification and I sensed the loss of any transient definition my life briefly held that summer.

"Rex, you stopped me telling you," she said.

"So I ran here from all the parties."

"It was the last one you gave. You owed drug money. Although you'd stopped, you still had a ready supply for your guests. There was a particularly nasty piece of work after you, Al. The guests had left when he arrived, long after midnight."

"Why didn't I pay him?"

"You argued with him. Someone had complained about the quality of the coke, you thought he was selling you substandard gear."

"Where was Eve?"

"She was there. So was I. You were outside by the pool with Al. You threatened him, you said you'd get him hurt. He'd brought along a heavy and he wasn't going to lose face. You were yelling at him. I was standing at the door to the house and Eve ran towards you, she was frightened he was going to hurt you. The last word she uttered was 'Stop'. I can still hear it. Al pulled a gun and you grabbed it. It went off, over your shoulder, killing Eve."

42.

It seemed my world stopped with Eve's last breath. Suddenly the memory of the sniper shots and the falling Zippo became more real as I learned the truth of what had happened. I must have merged the memory with the image of Coral's lighter.

As she lit a cigarette, I said, "Did you drop that when it happened?"

Her eyes were fixed on the black and hollow plasma screen.

"I did."

"What happened to the killer?"

"He left."

"No police?"

"Rex, the house was full of drugs. I had to call an ambulance."

"But she was dead."

"Yes. As you turned to see what had happened, Al struck you across the head with the butt of his gun and left. You suffered severe head damage and memory loss. That's why you can't remember anything. The doctor who saw you said you wouldn't have any recollection of that night's events. When I'd got rid of the evidence I called the police. They went to question Al, but he was already dead."

"Who killed him?"

"Why do you assume someone killed him? He drove into the path of a lorry and his car was thrown off the road. He and his heavy died in a burning Merc."

"Did they investigate?"

"They found the gun in the car and matched it to the bullet in Eve."

"I've remembered pieces, but they're disconnected, as if the images don't belong to me."

Her face looked unreal as she said, "You kept her pictures because you knew."

"Knew what?"

"You mustn't feel guilty, Rex."

"I think I can remember the party."

"Retrograde amnesia, Rex, that's what you're suffering from."

43.

I discovered that retrograde amnesia is memory loss of events that occurred just before a trauma or injury. I'd lost more than summer because of it.

Coral began to fill in the blanks for me. She told me about the life I led and the man I was.

She became my memory. I allowed her to paint the world for me. And she did it in the colours of her choosing. My daughter's face stared at me out of the darkness. Her accusing eyes woke me in the night.

The static shots of her that adorned my living room seemed empty of meaning. I'd placed them there as a reminder of forgotten things, a tie to someone I sought.

As Coral spoke I felt overwhelmed by loss. And it occurred to me that as I'd trained the camera on Evangeline, the film I made was focused on the past, and it wasn't Coral I sought but myself.

Absence of knowledge feels like a wound when it is yourself who is unknown. For Evangeline and Coral were like mirrors. And my image as reflected in them was empty of resonance. I searched Coral's face for answers, but every time I looked at her she seemed to wear the same expression.

"Eve was beautiful," she said the next day as I struggled to eat lunch.

"What happened before she was killed that night?"

"She'd been hanging out with some of the guests as she often did. You were too busy filming. She met some people a girl of her age shouldn't be exposed to."

"Did they harm her?"

"No, Rex, I kept an eye on her, as much as I was able to. But there were too many people to keep track of. She loved you, I sometimes think she loved you better than me."

As I wondered why she said this, Coral's face looked like a mask. I stared at her expression, and it seemed devoid of dimension, as if she'd set it to represent a single message.

"There's so much I've forgotten," I said.

"You just left everything."

"I remember the house."

"You know you're a wealthy man? You left your career hanging, Rex. You were searching for the next star. You wanted to make a film about two women competing with one another, that's all I know. You were obsessive about the kind of look you wanted. Your films were good, Rex, really good."

"One thing that must be embedded in me is filming. I bought a camera here, I've been taking films."

"Of?"

"Of you."

"Rex, you need help. I'm traumatised by what happened, that's why my stab at a marriage failed. I have to take pills sometimes to stop the memory of her dead body. It's funny, you can't remember and I want to forget."

I slumped into a chair. My stomach was convulsing, and the room blurred.

"I'm responsible for my daughter's death. Help me understand what happened, Coral."

She laid a hand on my shoulder.

"Rex, addictions come in many forms. You used to film me, remember?"

It all made sense, my films of Evangeline, the meetings in which I searched for the woman who now sat in my house. And it was as if Evangeline didn't exist. There had been no more parties and I hadn't seen her. I felt a prisoner in my studio home and left Coral sitting there.

I hadn't been outside for days, and I stepped onto my drive. The recollection of the first time I saw Evangeline entered my mind and it all seemed rehearsed, as if she'd been set there to make me recall the thing that still evaded me. Coral's description of Eve's death was taking shape in my mind, but I felt disconnected from it, as if it was part of someone else's narrative.

Broadlands Avenue was unchanged. And empty. There was no one on the pavements, there were no cars on the drive next door. I looked at the Glass's house. No lights. It all looked like a film set. And everything was arid, from the ground to the people, who seemed like desiccated shells, their sap removed by the violent sun. I wondered if Evangeline was with Michael, alive and fulfilled, or whether she'd taken Coral there and it was her Michael was penetrating in the heat.

They were no more than images to me. Those emotions which cause the most struggle between a man and a woman are the fundamental building blocks of our humanity. Without jealousy there may exist no passion. I was a voyeur lost in amnesia, and now I'd found the woman I'd been searching for and she horrified me. She horrified me with her words and the single look she bore that I began to analyse, as if it held a clue to the past.

44.

Coral showed me the man I was. My daughter died because of my lifestyle. I learned how I'd failed as a father, that the single skill I possessed was making films. Her revelations induced unbearable headaches, and I would lie holding my hands to my temples, wanting it to end.

I hated the heat. I revisited Eve's death scene in my mind, feeling empty, indicting myself with negligence and despising my films. I considered the nature of coral. I considered its durability and chief usefulness in making jewelry. Its intense pink colour seemed the hue of sex, lurid and exposed like erotic lips.

Coral's mouth was ever poised to speak, or suck the smoke from her Marlboro. She was an open invitation, but she beckoned me to the shadows. Her cigarette seemed permanently lit, filling my house with an odour I detested. Sometimes at night I thought I heard her talking in low tones, and imagined her consoling herself for a loss whose pain she bore alone. She had a secret language from which I was excluded. The things she told me became a code, and I wanted to crack Coral.

I wandered my garden in the dark. Shepperton was silent. The house next door seemed abandoned, as if its occupants had played their part in the drama. I lived in an abject state of self-disgust. Words of consolation were empty.

One morning she found the X. I'd placed it in a cupboard when she arrived.

"Film me," she said, handing it to me.

"You sound like Evangeline."

"And who is she?"

"Your living counterpart."

She ignored the comment that slipped from my mouth like a broken tooth. She viewed me as a troubled man who made little sense. And she was assured of her pre-eminence. Evangeline didn't exist that day as Coral played the part I'd assigned to the wrong woman.

She led me upstairs to the bedroom. We hadn't made love since that first time. The act had seemed to shed any desire between us and my interest in her was gone with the revelation she'd brought with her.

"This is how you used to like it, Rex," she said.

Coral stripped, slowly, methodically, eyeing the camera all the time. I felt as though she was peering beyond the lens, her image searing the film.

Her body looked different as I filmed it. Her body seemed cheap, and her entire sexuality looked meretricious. She lay on the bed and spread her legs, her focus on the camera. I put the X down.

I took her breasts in my hands and tasted her lips. I entered her hungrily and swallowed the hollow seeds of her mouth. I needed to show her I existed. I wanted to penetrate her to her sleeping core. I was a participant now, and I left her sweating on the bed.

45.

I was losing definition again. The brief sketch I'd drawn of Rex had been erased by Coral's accounts of my negligence as a father.

I became preoccupied by filming Coral in the same way as I had been with Evangeline. And I struggled to define some key distinction between the two women.

I watched the old films while Coral slept. I saw that Evangeline looked alive in ways that Coral didn't. There was something missing in Coral. On film her face looked flat and expressionless, and it occurred to me she only had one expression.

I would lie awake at night trying to define what I was seeing. My perceptions seemed untrustworthy.

I was living in a shadow land of amnesia into which fractured memories broke through. For I was remembering bit by bit. Episodes of parties came to me, as did the brief smell of cocaine in the stagnant Shepperton air. I was getting fragments of the past back, but they were disjointed scenes in a broken reel of film.

Names and faces entered my mind, snapshots of people and phrases I'd once known. One of them was the Kuleshov Effect. I Googled it one static midnight. I knew about films, I knew a lot.

The Russian film maker Lev Kuleshov had made a film using Tsarist matinee idol, Ivan Mosjoukine in the 1920s. He took a single shot of the actor's expressionless face and juxtaposed it next to various images. The acting was lauded, and the film maker realised that audiences come with their own emotional responses to visual prompts, which they then attribute to the actor.

That day I realised that Coral was the living embodiment of the Kuleshov Effect, a woman with one expression, whose beauty enticed me to fill her words and gestures with emotions that were entirely lacking in her.

On film Evangeline was expressive and had a range of looks. When Coral spoke of our daughter, there was no change in her appearance. She had no sorrow and she had no heart.

If she had one expression, then applying the Kuleshov Effect might reverse that and bring her to life. Film showed how static she was. To test my theory I took a shot of her with the Nikon that day. It was of her face as she sat to eat breakfast. Her mouth was closed and she was looking at her food with that same look she brought to everything.

I juxtaposed the picture with a range of images and she came alive. I set it against the picture of Eve, and Coral seemed full of grief and heartache.

But the emotions were not hers, they were mine, and I knew she was tricking me.

46.

I wanted to excavate the truth of her. I filmed her while she slept, her bare legs thrown over the spare bed, her face turned to the darkness. She seemed set against aging and all its changes. It was as if she'd been born with a mask and over the ensuing days I wanted to remove it. I imagined tearing her skin away to find an implacable and unyielding image there. I slept with her twice during that time. I dwelt on the falsity of her bodily promise, the calculated deceit with which she feigned pleasure. And I realised that the single look she bore was part of her need to control every effect.

I stared at my tired face in the empty mirror. I was a man who could not be part of life, who took images and let his daughter die while he fled to the land of amnesia with a camera. The sorrow Coral's disclosure released was agonising. I wandered my house unwashed, drunken, contemplating a way to end it all. I could barely look at Eve's picture. Her eyes accused me from the frames.

And then, one night, I rose to get some water. The sky felt on fire.

Passing into the hall, I heard Coral talking on her mobile.

"Have you put it in my name yet? Yes, I know how you feel, but consider the alternative."

I regained my room before she knew I was listening.

47.

As she slept, I went into her phone and found the last dialled number. I noted it down and called it from my mobile, withholding my number.

Francis Merit's voice was as familiar to me as if I'd spoken to him the day before. I had no image of him in my mind but I recognised his tone, its suave insincerity, his menace as he said, "Who is this?" It was in the accent, it was in the slow serpentine hiss in the silence that ensued that my buried knowledge of the past lay. In that vacuum of sound where speech ended I wanted to harm him and I didn't know why. Guilt overwhelmed me again as I ended the call.

I stood for a long time afterwards in the silent hallway. A woman was sleeping upstairs, she was a key to my lost memories, and I couldn't trust her.

I went into the garden and listened for life next door. It was as if Evangeline no longer existed. My life was staged, the events since I arrived at Broadlands Avenue part of someone else's direction. I wanted to break out of the endless film.

The next morning I forced myself to take a shower. I watched Coral over breakfast. She fitted in with the sterile furniture of my house, and I considered that it was this feature, the sterility of our existence, our lost child, that gave her the stasis I'd noticed a few days before.

"How long do you plan to stay?" I said.

"I have nowhere else to go."

"What about Francis? Can't you make it work?"

"I never want to talk to him again."

The reason she lied so well is that there was no distinguishing look to judge her by. She only had one look.

48.

I began to wonder if there were hidden cameras in the walls. I imagined million of lenses secreted in Broadlands Avenue. Coral treated The Telescope as if it was hers. Her things were strewn around the house. She set her i Pod up in the living room. Her cigarette smoke hung in the air. I wanted to get rid of her.

I went upstairs and looked at the bed on which I'd made love to three women. The extreme fascination of disgust overwhelmed me. Each sexual act, each exchange of bodies existed in the uses we'd set for one another. I could see Samantha lying beneath me with supplicating eyes as I plundered her for information. Entering Evangeline was like turning the key in the lock, I heard gunshots in her groans, and saw smoke rise from her arching hips. She wasn't Coral, even when she played her, she lacked her body's deceit. Coral was watchful in bed, and when penetrated seemed to be calculating the level of my desire.

But I knew where my desire lay. And I wondered if Coral sensed her in the shadows. Coral was a replica, Evangeline the original. I'd thought it was the other way around. I considered the best way of getting her out of my house.

I stepped onto the drive that evening and saw two cars. Harry and Evangeline were at home. Everything came into focus then.

I went back inside The Telescope and found Coral drinking wine in the kitchen. I poured myself a glass. The house was baking in the heat and the walls seemed to be cracking, as if the physical world stood on the verge of a revelation and was about to show its immateriality. I heard a door slam and a car drive off.

"Rex, there are still some things you don't remember," Coral said, "things I am not sure I should tell you."

"Why would you keep them from me?"

"I don't know if you're ready to hear them yet."

"What could be worse than what you've already told me?"

She turned that single glance on me and was about to say something when the door bell rang.

I went to answer it.

It was Evangeline, and I took her into the living room. Her eyes were heavy, as if she hadn't slept.

"Harry's found out," she said.

"About us?"

"About me and Michael. He hired a detective. I don't know how much else he knows. That's why I haven't been around. I couldn't risk it. I've had to watch my every move. I knew someone was following me a few days ago, but last night Harry showed me the pictures."

"Does he know whose baby it was?"

"He assumes it was Michael's. He drove off just now. He came back to pack and he's gone. He's divorcing me."

"I'm sorry."

"It gets worse. I went to see Michael yesterday to break it off, hoping I could save my marriage. Harry had him beaten up. He's a mess, his nose is broken, he looks dreadful."

As she stood there she looked exiled.

"Do you want Michael?" I said.

"He won't have anything to do with me now, blames me for the attack, he's furious I got found out. They've both rejected me, Rex."

"What do you want, Evangeline?"

"I want you, Rex."

I smelt Coral's Marlboro before I heard her voice.

"Do you?" she said, leaning against the door frame, "I imagine a woman like you finds rejection hard to bear."

It was bizarre standing there, looking at both of them. They didn't belong in the same room, let alone the same world. I felt as though I was staring into a mirror, Coral reflecting Evangeline, and that only one of them was real.

They were not identical. On examination, you could see that Evangeline had a fuller figure, moved more gracefully, and of course, that Coral had one expression. But their faces, and the colour of their hair were almost the same.

The green of their eyes differed. Coral's were darker, harder, and Evangeline's had a depth to them I still hadn't fathomed.

As Coral stepped across the threshold, it was obvious that the two women hated each other on sight.

"Is this her?" Evangeline said.

"This is Coral."

Coral jutted her chin at Evangeline.

"Who's she?"

"My next door neighbour."

"The name's Evangeline, and I'm more than that."

"Are you indeed?" Coral said.

Her cigarette was burning down and she stood there without taking her eyes off Evangeline. I watched the feather of ash hang, as the red tip almost reached her fingers.

"Are you filming her too?" Evangeline said.

I didn't answer her.

Coral stubbed out her Marlboro and turned to me, dismissing Evangeline.

"Perhaps you'd like to tell me what's been going on."

49.

They both stood there looking at me.

"It seems to me, Coral, that you are giving me an account of myself."

"What does that mean?" Coral said.

"It means that ever since you turned up you have handed me a version of myself, your version of myself."

Evangeline had missed an act in the drama and she was not going to be dismissed so easily. She got in between us.

"He wanted me to play you," she said to Coral.

"Play me?"

"He said he wanted me to act Coral."

"And what did that involve?"

"He didn't know who you were, I had to find you. And for the last months he has filmed me."

"Coral is the mother of my daughter."

"Then why didn't you know who she was, Rex? Or is this some elaborate sick game of yours?"

"He's suffering from amnesia," Coral said.

"Why is she back, Rex?"

"I'm here to help him."

"And why do I suspect your help is not without a price?"

The two of them had set the stage for their drama. I was a redundant actor and watched as they tried to upstage one another.

"Did he try fucking you too, Evangeline?"

"He did fuck me."

"Or was it me he sought in your body?"

"I would know the difference."

I could see them transposing all those parts of themselves they detested to each other. I thought of the lie, of the call to Francis Merit. Evangeline was real, and Coral was a fabrication, something from my past that refused to yield the thing I'd sought.

"What claim does she have on you, Rex?" Coral said.

"Why do you think she has a claim on me?"

They both looked at me. In that moment I hated them, the two fictions carved from vanity and deceit. I wanted them removed. I couldn't answer them, even my name was foreign to me. Everyone pretends. Until they can't anymore.

"Are you going to tell her, or am I?" Evangeline said.

"Tell me what?" Coral said.

PRIVATE GAMES

50.

Evangeline kept her eyes fixed on Coral's as she answered her.

"A few weeks ago I was carrying his child."

If Coral had an expression other than the permanent one etched into her face it may have flickered briefly into life then as she turned to me.

"Is this true, Rex?"

I walked away from them, and drank wine in the kitchen while they raised their voices in the other room.

That was where it lived, in the other room, away from me, this thing I'd sought and now found odious and repellent. My daughter was dead and I would never have another.

They followed me, as if their futures lay in my empty sweating hands that cooled themselves on the glass. I could feel Coral's breath on my neck as I looked away from her, through the window, to the garden and the fountain at its end.

"Rex, after what happened, I deserve to know the truth."

"What happened?" Evangeline said.

"He killed our daughter."

"What?"

"Now Coral, you are giving yourself away," I said.

"It was as good as murder. Rex liked to entertain people, with drugs. Eve was shot by a man he owed money to."

"I don't remember any of this."

"I bet you don't," Coral said.

There was venom in her voice and her eyes were textured like snake's skin as she looked at me.

I went to get a painkiller for my throbbing head. When I returned Evangeline was standing inches from Coral. The world seemed a proposition of parallel truths and lies as I looked at the two of them, like Siamese twins locked in mutual hatred.

"If he's suffering from amnesia how can you be trusted?" Evangeline said.

"Why did you call Francis Merit the other night, Coral?" I said.

"I did no such thing."

"I saw the evidence on your phone."

"So you're snooping on me now?"

"I heard the call."

Coral turned to Evangeline.

"He probably snooped on you too."

"You're not answering my question," I said.

"You know he used to get obsessed by a certain type of woman. Star quality, he called it. Rex is a filmmaker, did you know that?

"Doesn't surprise me."

"I had the look, I still do, Rex, based on your performance in bed the other night." She glanced at Evangeline as she said this. "I remember before you left you'd been looking for another one of your stars. He may have even come here and seen you in the street, taken a few shots. Is that why you bought this house, Rex? Because she was here and you could play your sick game?"

I couldn't remember why I bought The Telescope, or even visiting it. I could only recall that day when I left Richmond and came there, and the first time I saw her on the drive, as if she'd been placed in Broadlands Avenue for all of this to unfold.

"I think it's you who's playing a game, Coral."

But she wouldn't look at me, only at Evangeline.

"Do you believe this man, who comes here with two pictures of his dead daughter and films you?"

"I'm not going to believe what you want me to."

"Why did you call Francis if it's all over between you?" I said.

"There are still things to sort out."

"Like me?"

"It didn't work between me and Francis because I can't have children, not after Eve."

"So you're barren," Evangeline said.

My wine smelt of blood as I swirled it in the glass and drank it to the dregs.

51.

The winning card Evangeline held was her pregnancy and she'd tossed it away. I thought I saw regret worm its way into her face.

They were fighting for their identities. Stars need space to shine and no two stars enjoy being placed too close together.

Coral went to get more cigarettes from the spare room, leaving me alone with Evangeline.

"I've nothing left, Rex, I can't have her here," she said. "I risked my marriage for you. And now I've lost it."

"Harry's left you because of Michael, not us."

"The only reason he became suspicious is because of her. Acting Coral altered me in some way, that's what made Harry think I was having an affair. And now she's here. Who do you want?"

"I want you, Evangeline."

"Why, if I'm just another woman who looks like her?"

"Because you taught me what desire is."

Coral was standing in the hall as we spoke, and she came back into the kitchen.

"She'll have to go, Rex, you can't have both of us."

"Will I?" Evangeline said.

"I think you're lying to me, Coral."

"About what?"

"Everything, the whole account of how Eve died, I don't think that's how it happened at all."

"Rex, you remember the shots, why would I make this up?"

"Because you want something out of him," Evangeline said.

She did.
She wanted it all.

52.

Perhaps it was that word, "shots", which prompted the slow release of numerous triggers in my mind. Perhaps. But what ensued was like witnessing a series of fireworks going off in my head. Images bombarded me over the next twenty-four hours, pictures of myself and Eve in the past, and all of it felt unreal. Amnesia is like losing your sense of touch. You can still feel the physical presence of objects, but they have lost their shape and texture. Your memories haunt you. But they do not belong to you. Coral and Evangeline, the two women locked in battle, my time at The Telescope, the death of my daughter, all of it belonged in some alienated place that resonated with the inner emptiness that had consumed me for as long as I could remember.

It is interesting to note the same word is used on film sets. And that is the medium that led me to myself. Through filming Evangeline I'd found fragments of the past. I wondered how many shots I'd taken of both women, and how many shots the detective took of Evangeline before he had enough evidence to hand to Harry.

He had indentified the thing that Harry suspected, and I had been trying to identity myself. Identity. It is wrapped up in body image, in status, in so many small things that lead to acts we hide. Everyone hates themselves at some point in their lives. No matter what our attributes are, no matter what our looks or abilities are, there is a stage in our development where our narcissism balks at accepting our identity. I loathed myself during those days when the reality that I was responsible for Eve's death took hold of my mind. I watched Evangeline's and Coral's self-loathing as they saw themselves in each other.

"It was me he wanted," Coral said to Evangeline.

"Do you still want her now, Rex?" Evangeline said to me.

I wanted the past.
I wanted myself back.

53.

They'd climbed inside the lens. They'd invaded The Telescope and vied for pre-eminence. They needed that above all else. They wanted to see their own reflections, but not in each other.

I wondered, that torrid night when Broadlands Avenue slept through the heat, which one would win. The answer should have been obvious.

I was left alone with Evangeline at one point, when Coral went upstairs. I heard her opening cupboards and I hoped this bearer of truths was packing her things.

"Rex, I know how much you wanted me in bed," Evangeline said.

"I wanted you all along."

"Get rid of her."

I went upstairs and found Coral searching through my drawers.

"You want my money?" I said.

"I'm trying to find something."

"Among my affairs?"

"Interesting choice of word, Rex."

"Is that what you think Evangeline is?"

"I hold the key to you, Rex. There's a lot I haven't told you, things that could push you over the edge."

"Try me."

"Show me the films."

54.

When I went downstairs Evangeline had left. I could see lights on next door. They reminded me of those early summer days when I stood listening to her parties.

Then I smelt Coral's smoke. She was standing behind me waiting, and I led her through to the living room, where I played her the first of the films.

"Why are you showing me this?" she said.

"I assume you want to see how well she played you."

I saw her face harden as she noticed her rival assume her character, as if I'd been preparing her to steal Coral's identity. And perhaps I had in a way. Perhaps, knowing how much erosion of my own identity had occurred, I knew my only defence against what was to come was to have a substitute waiting in the wings.

She spent hours studying the creation. And when she began to tire of the endless scenes of Evangeline dressed as her, she turned to me and said, "She's not me, you know."

"I know."

"You needed me because I know all about you, Rex."

"I'm not sure I want your version of me."

That was the moment when I knew I was staring into a mirror. That's all she was. There was no depth to her eyes. There was no way of reading her face. She was beautiful. She was Coral. She was a liar. And I saw what I wanted to in the canvas of her eyes. I will never know if she read that moment for what it was, the end of her reign.

"You have other films in the house," she said.

The doorbell rang and I left the room. It was Evangeline, and I let her in. She was swaying slightly, and I could smell wine on her breath as she said, "I went to check my messages. Harry's cut off my finances."

She wandered into the living room.

"So, it's the money," Coral said to her. "How much to get rid of you?"

"That might be what brought you here, but that's not why I want Rex."

There was a moment when I wished the X was running. To have captured it from behind the lens would have given me a recording. Now I rely on my memory. Both women brought out their lighters. The two Diva Zippos mirrored one another as the Swarovski crystals in the burnished surfaces caught the light. I have never seen such hatred.

"Was this some plan on your part to replace me, Rex?" Coral said.

"It's a lighter, Coral, that's all it is."

"Is yours engraved? You see what mine says?" Coral held it up to Evangeline's face. "To my favourite star."

"I don't think you are any longer," Evangeline said.

"Why do you want Rex?"

"I don't have to explain myself to you. I think now he's seen you he's disappointed. The thing I found out about you when I acted you is that you're a game player."

"You just discovered yourself on film."

"How can Rex believe what you say?"

"You know him, do you? Know how he snorted coke every night, had orgies, filmed all the naked bodies? You're just another one of them. I had his child."

"And what did happen to her?"

"That's right, Coral, what did happen to Eve?" I said.

She looked at me and took a deep drag on her cigarette.

"I don't trust you one little bit," Evangeline said.

And neither did I. And I knew she was not what I'd searched for. The one thing she'd said that was the truth was that she held a key. But she would never give it to me.

"What is it you want from Rex?" Evangeline said.

Coral turned on her iPod, no doubt wanting to drown her out. Fleetwood Mac's "The Chain" reverberated into the room.

With Coral there and the song playing I felt as though a huge wave had submerged me and I was tipping backwards in space and time. Fragments of the past flickered into life. The two women began to argue. And I walked away. I went upstairs and shut myself in the spare room to drown out the noise and pack up Coral's things. But the image of the falling Zippo and the sound of gunshots played over and over in my mind.

As I opened the cupboard I saw some boxes I'd left unpacked. Inside them were films. They were labelled and most were studio takes. But there was one that was unmarked. It contained a note.

"Dad, this will show you why I did it," it read.

I knew it was Eve's hand.

ON FILM

55.

I removed the disc and watched the film, while beneath me Evangeline and Coral argued. They were contesting a prize that had already been lost. I could hear their voices faintly in my bedroom, as I saw my daughter come alive again briefly on the video she'd left for me. And what she gave me in the film was reality, and its questionable comfort. I wonder now whether I would have preferred to remain in amnesia. What I found out changed everything. It changed summer.

The film itself was a wounding account of that night's events as they occurred. That night I was erased. I'd sought a new Rex in Broadlands Avenue, while amnesia wiped out my ability to perceive correctly, until I watched that film. And what I gained was something I didn't want to know.

Eve's face flickered onto the screen. Her eyes were heavy with crying, her voice broken, as she spoke into her camcorder. The pictures in the living room suddenly came to life.

"Dad, I've hidden the video in your box of Diva's Descent. I don't want you to blame yourself, I know what the need for drugs is like. But I can't live with a mother who would do this to me. I got into coke to stop the creeps, it gave me courage. For a while. That argument you had tonight, when she said she was leaving you for Francis. Well, she's got him where she wants him. It's good you have cameras everywhere because I have the film, go and watch what she's done to me. She left me alone with him, while I was comatose, and now she's blackmailing him. I can't live like this. I don't want to live like this."

It ended there. I knew that Diva's Descent was one of my films. I found the box and the unmarked disc. It was the hardest film I have ever had to watch.

It was shot by one of the covert cameras I'd placed everywhere in the house in Richmond. The first image was of Eve asleep on the bed in the spare room. A man entered the room, his back to the camera. He approached the bed and lifted the covers. Eve's naked legs. He turned and I saw Francis Merit's face. He removed his trousers.

She stirred in her sleep as he entered her. She was screaming by the time he finished, before he clamped his hand over her mouth. Afterwards, Eve tried to get away from him, but he grabbed her wrist. He chopped some lines and held her face down to the mirror.

Then Coral entered the room. She walked up to him and slapped him, said something and left.

My stomach was convulsing as I watched the rape of my daughter by the man Coral had left me for.

It was all coming back. As I vomited in the bathroom, the flushing water of the toilet terrified me, inducing a cold sweat that was still running down my back when I went downstairs.

THE SHOWDOWN

56.

They were still arguing, their voices louder, more insistent. The music had stopped and Evangeline was standing inches away from Coral's face.

"I don't believe a word," she said.

"Neither do I," I said.

Coral turned and sneered at me as I walked over to her.

"Eve committed suicide because of you. I found the video she left."

"What video?"

I poured myself a glass of wine to steady my shaking hands.

"The video where she is asleep and Francis rapes her."

"You really do need help."

"Come upstairs and I'll play it to both of you."

She looked away.

Coral tried. She did her best, she slumped onto the sofa and said, "I was trying to keep it from you, Rex, it's true, he raped her, that's why I left him."

"You knew."

"I only found out last week."

"I saw you enter the room where our daughter lay drugged and you slapped his face after he'd done it. You knew what had happened and you still left with him."

"That's outrageous."

Evangeline was watching as I tore Coral's mask from her face.

"Eve left a video for me in which she recounts how you set her up with Francis, how you watched him rape her to blackmail him."

There was a momentary pause as she tried to calculate her next lie. And I knew that I'd found the truth in an unpacked box. I had everything I needed with me when I arrived at The Telescope, except the thing I needed the most wasn't labelled.

"She was sick in the head. I had to spend hours talking to her about her fantasies. She thought men were after her. They made moves on me all the time, Rex, those parties attracted a bad crowd and once or twice I found men trying it on with Eve, but the truth is she didn't have it, she never would, she lived in the shadow of your stars and that is why she lied."

"It's all Rex's fault, isn't it?" Evangeline said.

Coral turned to her.

"That's right."

"You're lying."

"I'm beginning to remember," I said.

Evangeline looked at me.

"What do you remember, Rex?"

I could hear "The Chain," the steady guitar riff fetching images from the deep, and bringing reality back.

"That song was playing. You used to play it all the time. We'd been arguing. You told me you wanted to leave me and then the party started."

"You have amnesia Rex, you don't know what you're talking about," Coral said.

"I had retrograde amnesia caused by trauma and I'm recovering my memory."

"What happened, Rex?" Evangeline said.

"I knew Coral was unfaithful, I knew she slept around. She and Francis were talking in a corner of the pool room, I heard them whisper something. I walked outside and saw it. Eve's body floating in the pool."

That was when my fear of water ended. It was clear that all my fears and obsessions since I'd arrived with half a memory at The Telescope were my body's way of leading me back to the place where I'd lost a piece of myself, that night I lost my daughter.

Coral lit a cigarette.

"That is not what happened," she said.

"What did she do? Lie down to sleep in the pool, drugged out of her head?"

"She was shot, Rex."

But I knew it in her eyes. I knew the shadow of the lie that had always dwelt there, the reason she never changed expression.

"What have you really come back for, Coral?" Evangeline said.

"Money," I said.

"I left Francis because of what he did."

"I'll tell you what I think happened, Coral," I said. "I think you were jealous of Eve, her beauty. I remember Francis, the kind of women he liked. You knew you were too old for him, you saw he wanted Eve. You can't stand competition. You let him be alone with her. You wanted him to rape her. You blackmailed him."

"So why have I left him?"

"Something hasn't worked out."

"Do you think this would-be star is the answer?"

"I knew you when I played you," Evangeline said. "I changed as I became you for a while. There is nothing you would stop at, Coral, you have no morals."

"You're an impostor, I know Rex."

"I don't want you here, Coral," I said. "If you don't want money, pack your bag and leave."

But she wasn't going anywhere.

I went into the kitchen to pour more wine. It was all coming back, the images crystal sharp and as clear as only reality can be. I saw the party, the men and women gathered at the house. And I saw Eve floating in the pool.

Evangeline came into the room and held out her glass.

"Why are you fighting for me?" I said. "I filmed you without you wanting me to. I found out your affair. I made you play Coral."

"Because I lied, I'm not her, but we're both liars."

"What did you lie about?"

"I didn't abort it. I knew Harry was getting suspicious and when he saw the pregnancy kit I decided to get rid of it. But I couldn't. I told you Harry was sterile, it isn't true. He doesn't want kids, he's said to me for years if I lost my figure he'd leave me. I'm getting older Rex. I stood in the clinic and decided I wasn't going to do what Harry wanted. I have to look the way he wants me to. He tries to choose what I wear. That's why it was easy going along with your films, dressing up for the part of Coral. And something strange happened. Some intimacy grew between us. I told you things I haven't told anyone. I tried to see if I could throw Harry off the scent, make him think it was his child. It's too late, it's yours and I want it."

Coral had come up behind her.

"Are you really going to believe this whore?" she said.

144

57.

Evangeline had made the challenge. And it all revolved around Eve. At the heart of the film were my drowned daughter and the second child swimming in amniotic fluid.

Coral was lighting a cigarette. I watched her snap the Zippo shut and remembered myself standing behind the camera. The falling lighter and the sound of the gunshots were in the last scene of Diva's Descent. I'd held onto a memory of one of my films as an explanation for the loss I felt.

"She wasn't shot, I know what happened."

"Rex, you don't know," Coral said.

"I do. The memory is of Diva's Descent."

"You've filmed so much you don't know what's real anymore," Coral said, putting her lighter back in her bag.

"I gave you that. It was used by the actress in the film."

She looked away.

"Who was the actress, Rex?" she said.

"It doesn't matter."

"Rex used to ask me what would Coral do?" Evangeline said. "And I know now, she would get her daughter raped just to secure the man she'd set her sights on."

Coral slapped her then. It was a hard slap and Evangeline glared at her.

I remembered what Samantha had told me about her.

"I gave you the lighter. You came off a film set."

I will never forget the look on Coral's face as I said that. It was the closest thing to wounded she could muster.

"We both lost a daughter, Rex."

"And how deeply have you been cut? You only have one look, Coral. There is a range of expressions in Evangeline's face."

"Why do you think you've got amnesia, Rex?" she said. "Al knocked you out after he shot Eve."

"I had an argument with Francis."

PARTIES AND PILLS

58.

It was all about Eve. It was about reproducing, and loss, and lies and the need to stamp their image on time. Time had stopped until that night when it moved backwards and I knew it all again. And Evangeline wanted to rid herself of that seed of self-loathing the film had germinated in her soul, like a rotten replica, viral and aggressive in her character.

"I was standing by the pool looking at her body floating there when he came out. 'Leave it to me, Rex,' he said. 'Why would I leave it to you?' Those words are clear in my head. He came towards me and I remember hitting him. I knew he'd been screwing you, we'd had a blazing row earlier that day. I didn't know he'd raped my daughter or I would have killed him. We fought. I remember he picked up a parasol. He was swinging the pole at me. That was how I got concussed and where my amnesia began."

Coral shook her head and turned to Evangeline.

"You don't want this man to have your child."

I went into the hall. I wanted to shut their voices out of my head and let the images settle in my mind. I wanted to dwell on my memories and secure a rope around reality's shaking sail. Eve's film had plugged right into the trauma and my amnesia was over. It was all coming back, places, people, events, conversations.

Coral was lying all right. I'd threatened to divorce her that day I found out about her and Francis. She set him up with Eve. She blackmailed him and now she'd come back to inflict her version of that night on me while she got my money. As I stood there I saw her mobile phone light up in her bag.

I listened to the message. It was from Francis.

"I can't go on," he said, "You holding this over me. I don't have the money and I don't have the desire. I'm not going to give you my house. I hope you find Rex's stash of cash, you're going to need it in your old age."

There was a set of keys at the bottom of her bag and I removed them.

I remembered where he lived. I got the keys to my car and drove to Kensington.

London was on fire that night as I sped through deserted streets. I parked outside his house and opened the front door.

The ground floor was empty. I scaled the stairs and saw his body from the hallway. He'd hanged himself from the bedroom cupboard. Francis Merit's face was closed to the world.

I drove back, aware that I rarely left the house, ready for the two fighting women at The Telescope.

59.

They were waiting for me, the arbiter of their stardom. I see them now, all those years ago, through the shattered lens of memory, two women with narcissism running through their veins like morphine.

"So you're back," Coral said, like an outraged wife arguing with her husband's mistress.

"I've seen the film," Evangeline said.

There was a broken wine glass in the corner of the room, its stem stood pointlessly on the carpet as it dripped Meursault onto the pile.

Evangeline came towards me.

"When you were out she went into the garden. I found the film upstairs, I watched it."

"What happened has nothing to do with you," Coral said. "You are an understudy."

"No, she was the star, she was always the star."

"Get out now and let me and Rex have a life," Evangeline said.

"You think you can get rid of me that easily?"

"Do you want to know where I went?"

"Looking for another star?" Coral said.

"I went to Francis's house, the one you shared with him while you milked him of money. He'd dead. He hanged himself."

"Another one of your insane lies, Rex. You're sick, you need help."

"He left a message on your phone, if you don't believe me, listen to it."

I went and got it and threw it at her.

Evangeline and I watched as she heard Francis's final words.

There was no sorrow in her face, no remorse as she turned her mobile off and put it on the sofa.

"You've killed two people," I said.

"On the film you came in and slapped him. You knew and you still went to live with him," Evangeline said.

"You were blackmailing Francis. You came here looking for the film so you could destroy it. You wanted his house. Well, you're not going to get it, and you're not going to get my money."

I could tell she had nothing left. In that moment she did change her expression and the static image of the posed actress fell away. Her face was filled with venom and deceit and I have never seen anything uglier than her in the few seconds when she realized she'd lost.

Dawn was breaking outside, as a pink light fell through the French doors. They'd been arguing through the night.

"Rex, I'm going to get some things from next door and then let's go to bed," Evangeline said.

I wished I'd stopped her. I went to pour a glass of wine and when I returned the front door was open and both of them were gone.

That was when I heard the scream. It was a piercing spontaneous cry that only pain produces.

I ran to the Glass's house. The front door was shut and I went down the passage.

As I came to the edge of the swimming pool Evangeline ran outside followed by Coral. Evangeline's face was bleeding. Coral grabbed her by the hair and Evangeline slapped her. I raced to the other side of the pool where they were fighting as Coral kicked Evangeline in the stomach.

"You're not having his child," Coral said.

As I got there Evangeline picked something up from the table by the pool and struck Coral across the head with it. Coral turned her face to me and her eyes were filled with a dying light like the sun at dusk.

She fell into the water. She sank beneath a large swelling rose of pink blood that streamed outwards from her head, face down to static eternity in the azure floodlit pool.

60.

Evangeline looked beautiful as they led her away. I will never know who called the police, but one of the watchful neighbours in Broadlands Avenue dialled the number as day began.

I considered how to dispose of Coral's body and protect Evangeline in the few minutes that elapsed after she killed her. She was standing there with the ashtray in her hand staring down into the pool. It was a heavy glass ashtray and a strand of Coral's hair hung from it. It sank into the water as Evangeline dropped it. I held her briefly in my arms and kissed her face one last time that lost and tortured summer when I found myself again and wished I hadn't. Then I heard the sirens and they came for her.

The heat was already overwhelming as I went next door and packed. My time at The Telescope was over.

I wished I was still filming her, there, alone, with Harry at work, discovering Coral forever as our sexual desire mounted like a flame. I considered what would have happened if Coral had never arrived.

And so I left. I gave the keys to the surprised agent who sold me the property and after a few days in a hotel moved into the new house in Bracknell. I made a good cash offer, and exchanged and completed on the same day. It is spacious and well lit. I am its history.

I visited Evangeline every week while she waited for the trial, and I sat in court throughout it. She miscarried during this time and I watched her fade with grief.

I gave my testimony, but the case against her was too strong. Harry's CCTV cameras had caught the fight.

They gave her six years for manslaughter. She had a previous criminal conviction for assault. She'd attacked a woman at a party many years before.

Her lawyer tried to use the mitigating factors of her pregnancy and the mental pressures that playing Coral had placed her under. The fact that it was not Harry's child didn't sit well with the jury, and her miscarriage weakened her case. I was asked for the films as evidence, but the removal men lost them when I left Broadlands Avenue. The prosecution lawyer made her look like a liar. He said she would have made a good actress. She is the only star in Holloway, immaculate in prison clothes.

* * *

Once when I visited her, I asked her what she planned to do when she got out.

"I'll be too old to have what I want," she said.

There was a moment when she looked cadaverous, as if being criminalised had hollowed her heart. She seemed in that instant like someone pretending to be Evangeline and I thought about the losses that summer, now over, had brought.

"What is it you want?" I said.

"You were right, Rex, I wanted to be a star. I was the star of my parties and the reason I fell into your trap is I was seduced by the attention. Coral was the same, that is why we clashed so drastically."

"She never had your scruples."

"No. And I was afraid to become like her."

"You'll still be a star when you get out."

"I'll be too old. Stardom is tied up in perpetual youth."

I looked at her, this prisoner, and I knew I had lied, that she would be too old to shine. Evangeline, beautiful, desirable Evangeline, corrupted by Coral, alone now.

"You may get a reduced sentence."

"I may. You know, my liberty was compromised when I first played Coral. You imprisoned me with the schedule of visits, turned me into someone else, made Harry suspect me."

"Don't you think he would have found out about you and Michael?"

"No, I don't, Rex. Because he wasn't following me around with a camera. Your knowledge of me, your accumulation of facts that I kept hidden, your constant poring over me like some specimen in a bottle, had removed my privacy. I was already naked before I stripped in front of you."

"What do you think would have happened if Coral hadn't come back?"

"I would have had your baby."

"What would you have told Harry?"

"I think it was over between us a long time before he left me. You know he's never tried to contact me since that night."

"You haven't heard from him since you've been in here?"

"No. Years ago I hit someone, Harry saw it, it frightened him. He needed to feel the dominant one. He told me it made me ugly and he hated it. It was a part of my character he wanted locked up. I guess you could say he got it."

There was a camera on the wall pointing down on us, and I wondered what fractured images it took then of our final meeting. I'd made her become someone else, someone I needed for my memory and identity, which I'd lost that summer. Evangeline was my way to the past, and I took away her future. I needed the continuity of time, and I found it in her face, and its simulations of Coral's. For without knowledge of the past we are lost, we are nothing, except the shadow of time on our lives.

I knew it was over then for Evangeline, and that when she got out she would be just another woman. Stars die. She was imploding. But there would be no supernova. I needed to enter the event horizon of a new discovery, I needed to penetrate another star.

And so I left her there, small and solitary.

"If you ever need anything," I said.

"I need myself, Rex."

The guards ushered me outside to the air and the open sky.

I caught a glimpse of her walking into the corridors that led to her cell.

I think of her there and imagine her smoking. I wonder who brings her cigarettes and if she uses her Zippo Diva lighter. Epiques do not seem to belong in prison. Neither do Swarovski crystals.

61.

I found out that Francis Merit had lied about his wealth. The detective I hired came back to me with bank statements showing he was not the source of income Coral had thought. Once she discovered this she began blackmailing him for his house. Her fatal prostitution of Eve had left her with nothing, not even life.

I managed to see the coroner's report. The finding for Eve Strike was death by suicide. She'd taken 26 Triazolam pills and drunk half a bottle of vodka before getting into the water. Cocaine was found in her system. There was no finding of rape. She died on the 12th of May.

I visited her grave a few weeks after Coral was killed. I bought some flowers and laid them on the earth and felt my tears on my cheeks as the rain began to fall. It was the day summer ended, and it seemed those endless weeks of sun belonged to another year.

I still think of Evangeline, locked away in prison. It's no place for a star, even a fading one. It's been a while since I visited her.

* * *

Harry tried to make contact with me via the estate agent some months after the trial. I didn't respond. I didn't want to give him my version of events. I didn't want his questions.

I saw him once standing outside a bar in London as I drove past. He looked sad and diminished, as if some fundamental equation in his character had been broken. Harry always existed on the margin of the drama, a man who liked to show off things that were not his.

62.

I watched Diva's Descent again the other day. It is as real as ever.

I see my hand hold the camera, all those years ago. I dwell behind the lens, detached and ruminative.

The final scene is perfect. The star is shot by the gunman secluded on the roof. She is smoking a Dunhill. The noise of the shots reverberates in the air. Her fingers are slender, erotic, as she clutches the lighter. Then they are gone as the bullets tear them from her hand. The falling Zippo burns its way into my mind.

Coral acted the part of the diva. She was my first star. The film captures the dying light in her eyes. It looks like a sunset on a bleeding ocean.

I pause the film as the credits roll. I think of her eyes in that final moment. They were the same as when she fell into the pool. And I consider that was what I sought all summer in another actress.

I contemplate my culpability in the drama. I wonder if Eve would be alive if I'd led a different life.

I remember it all now. I remember driving to Broadlands Avenue a few weeks before the party and the drowning. I'd seen Evangeline step from a shop in a floral dress in the beginnings of the heat. She stopped and looked at me and in that moment I knew she was a star in the making.

I followed her to her house and saw The Telescope was up for sale. It seemed an invitation. I knew that Coral was having an affair with Francis and wanted to leave. I needed another star, and so I set up my new life.

I bought The Telescope before I lost my memory. I went there with no knowledge of the events that led me there, as if I was simply following directions. But

I'd already found Evangeline. And there in the heat that felt like it would never end she played the part I'd set for her. I'd been planning the film for months.

On some level our knowledge exists beyond memory. And inasmuch as my instinct was to direct, Evangeline's was to act. She did it too well. She was not a replica. She had to kill her counterpart. I see her now, there, beneath me, naked and alone. I feel her body and its temperature rise.

I have pieced together as much as I can the events that were taken from me.

From what I can gather there was a drug dealer called Al. I know nothing more of his whereabouts. The story about what happened to him was no doubt one of Coral's fabrications. Everything she told me that summer was designed to cover up her culpability and to pour guilt into my amnesia.

The thing we call reality is made up of the strongest images that live in our minds. It is made up of memory, and if there is no past there is no future. And so we replace the details. In those months all I had was my film. Francis Merit's blow to my head had stolen yesterday and tomorrow, but I had my star.

I think of Evangeline, locked away in prison. She belongs in the heat and the light of that summer.

The weather has gone. The light has changed. I imagine she will be released one day. She exists in the constant climate of film.

People think I moved here to stay in the vicinity of a recording studio. The studio is everywhere.

The truth is there is another reason I chose this road. We are driven by a core. No matter what our conscious knowledge of it is, it guides our actions.

As I drove away from Shepperton that flaming summer, I saw her getting out of her car. Her pose and face were perfect. I followed her. I live a few doors away, but we have met. There are no parties here, she lives a different life to Evangeline, but I will find out the things I need to show her who she is.

I am going to get my camera, I think I will start filming again. I wonder how many days it will be before I manage to secure her time.

Each season erodes a piece of your identity. My stars outlive themselves on film. The camera sets me apart. It is the threshold on which I stand back and watch the seasons. The lens permits me to hold the world a little longer in my aging hands. I sometimes catch my reflection there, as I do on the glass face of my watch. I see the hour hand crawl across the finite circle of our lives.

Coral is timeless. I am left with the distance from time.

About the Author

Richard Godwin is the author of critically acclaimed novels *Apostle Rising, Mr. Glamour, One Lost Summer, Noir City, Meaningful Conversations* and *Confessions Of A Hit Man.*

One Lost Summer, published June 2013, is a Noir story of fractured identity and ruined nostalgia. It is a psychological portrait of a man who blackmails his beautiful next door neighbour into playing a deadly game of identity.

He is also a published poet and a produced playwright. His stories have been published in over 29 anthologies, among them his anthology of stories, *Piquant: Tales Of The Mustard Man.* He has also been published in *The Mammoth Book Of Best British Crime.*

Apostle Rising is a dark work of fiction exploring the blurred line between law and lawlessness and the motivations that lead men to kill. It digs into the scarred soul of a cop in the hunt for a killer who has stepped straight from a nightmare into the waking world.

Mr. Glamour is about a world of wealthy, beautiful people who can buy anything, except safety from the killer in their midst. It is about two scarred cops who are driven to acts of darkness by the investigation. As DCI Jackson Flare and DI Mandy Steele try to catch the killer they find themselves up against a wall of secrecy. And the killer is watching everyone.

Richard Godwin was born in London and obtained a BA and MA in English and American Literature from King's College London, where he also lectured.

You can find out more about him at his website, where you can also read his *Chin Wags At The Slaughterhouse,* his highly popular and unusual interviews with other authors.

www.richardgodwin.net